| WINTER CHILD |

l'enfant hiver

Virginia
Pésémapéo
Bordeleau

Winter Child

TRANSLATED BY
Susan Ouriou AND
Christelle Morelli

Translated with the support of the Canada Council for the Arts' translation
program. Published with the generous assistance of the Canada Council for
the Arts and the Alberta Media Fund.

Canada Council   Conseil des Arts   Alberta
for the Arts   du Canada   Government

Freehand Books
515 – 815 1st Street SW   Calgary, Alberta   T2P 1N3   www.freehand-books.com

Book orders: LitDistCo
100 Armstrong Avenue   Georgetown, Ontario   L7G 5S4
T: 1-800-591-6250   F: 1-800-591-6251   orders@litdistco.ca   www.litdistco.ca

Library and Archives Canada Cataloguing in Publication
Pésémapéo Bordeleau, Virginia, 1951–
[Enfant hiver. English]
Winter child / Virginia Pésémapéo Bordeleau ;
translated by Susan Ouriou and Christelle Morelli.
Translation of: L'enfant hiver.
Issued in print and electronic formats.   ISBN 978-1-988298-06-1 (softcover).
ISBN 978-1-988298-07-8 (EPUB).   ISBN 978-1-988298-08-5 (PDF)
I. Ouriou, Susan, translator   II. Morelli, Christelle, translator   III. Title.
IV. Title: Enfant hiver. English
PS8631.E797E5313 2017   C843'.6   C2017-900965-6   C2017-900966-4

Book design by Natalie Olsen, Kisscut Design
Cover image: Plate XIX of "Studies among the Snow Crystals ..." by Wilson
Bentley, 1902.
Author photo by Ariane Ouellet
Printed on FSC® recycled paper and bound in Canada by Marquis

For my son Simon
so that he may live
always

Is there life before death?

| UNKNOWN |

*Women never stop stitching men up
and men keep pouring themselves drinks.*

| MARIE UGUAY |

the cry

Her water broke in one swoosh, like a spring encased for too long in ice. The child would arrive soon, perhaps by day's end, her contractions coming faster by the hour. The pain hadn't yet begun. But intuition led her to phone the child's father and urge him to come home early from work and drive her to the village clinic. Her nerves thrummed with a tender feverishness; the birth would be uncomplicated, just as with her daughter, Amélie, whose arrival had been a moment of unspeakable joy, in keeping with her tiny being, her beauty so singular even then that the doctor and his assistant exclaimed together, "What a beautiful little girl!"

This time, they wheeled her into the delivery room as soon as she'd been examined. Her body was poised, she could feel the pressure of the baby's head, she pushed instinctively, urged on by the same nurse who'd been there for her first delivery. Her husband smiled valiantly at her; she could tell that he would gladly have taken on some of the pain of the baby's descent punctuated by her muffled moans. The doctor was close to retirement age and his face mask highlighted the wrinkles along his temples and under his eyes, accentuating the kindness of his gaze so like a grandfather's. Suddenly, he ordered, "Stop pushing!"

He shot a quick glance at the nurse, who handed him a pair of scissors. No words were exchanged, but the child's mother could tell something was wrong, she could read concern in the woman's eyes. The doctor remained expressionless, focused on the decision he had to make; she squeezed her husband's hand, held her breath, strove to fight off the panic threatening to engulf that space reserved for joy, for giving life; she squeezed her eyes shut and breathed deeply from the baby upwards, willing the baby to continue his journey through her.

The practitioner's fingers groped blindly inside her, then his words, "The cord is wrapped around the baby's neck, I'll have to cut now . . ."

She nodded.

His delicate gestures, the scissors disappearing inside, beads of perspiration pearling on his bald forehead, his intense focus on that opening, all shook her even further; she didn't want to see the expression on her husband's face, didn't want to lose heart by acknowledging the fear she sensed in him as the older man told her to push one last time. In one heave, she felt the child slide from her, damp and viscous, wetting her thighs. The moist heat of his body bursting from her womb fanned the hope that he would live; she caught a glimpse of his black hair matted with mucus, the blue tinge of his skin. The doctor laid him on her belly. His tiny, limp arms dangled on either side of her waist; she mouthed repeatedly, "My baby, my baby . . . ," while, still without a word, the doctor turned him, folded him over and over, reached a finger into his tiny mouth; the nurse handed him an instrument to aspirate the mucus. The child's mother stared at the gloved hands dancing across the tiny body, shaking him as though to waken him from sleep. The older man worked feverishly, bent on hearing the newborn's breath, until at last the baby uttered a first tentative croak like a frog unsure of spring's arrival. The child's father's tears. Her own silence in the icy grip of the interminable minutes of intimate terror, her womb still pulsating to the accelerated rhythm of her heart.

Snow fell and stayed. Winter made its entrance on that late September day. Come evening, a woman laid the child on her breast; clean and swaddled in a soft cotton blanket, he suckled hungrily. The woman smiled and said, "He's okay!"

Alone again, she cried, prayed as she laughed and directed a chorus of "thank yous" at the crucifix hanging on the wall across from her bed. Snow continued to fall, covering the window ledge; with the baby clasped to her breast, she let her gaze follow the falling snowflakes until her anguish eased.

A woman clad in pink stepped into the room. She carried clean towels, a washcloth, a small basin. When she untied the blue gown from behind your neck, your body was revealed. Your buttocks still youthful-looking, firm, still smooth, never exposed to the sun.

Could I have washed you? Ignored the taboo and touched my father's body? I don't think so. In any event, I didn't. Even knowing it should have been me, I didn't dare . . . Delicate throughout, the woman in pink caressed your face, dipped the washcloth into the basin of water, wrung it out and ran it gently over your skin. Respect brought moisture to your inert flesh, a hint of love's breath surrounded you because this woman, without knowing you, loved you.

You lay there, serene, handsome. If I die at your age, I know what my death will look like, my features like yours, like my son's, my daughter's and my granddaughter Léa who you never knew. For me, your departure came neither too soon nor too late; I was at peace with your leave-taking, there was nowhere left for the two of us to go, and yet part of the landscape collapsed before my eyes that morning to be replaced by a precipice. I was never able to speak the words you could never have accepted, given your boundaries, your padlocked doors, or maybe those bounds, those walls are my own . . . ? I inherited your position as the family's and clan's elder, no aunt or uncle lived longer than you; you left me at the crossroad between the road to maturity and that of childhood, a childhood that was mine as late as yesterday because you still lived. That morning I was no longer anyone's daughter, and my orphanhood rattled me: secretly, I had thought of you as immutable, there forever ahead of me, but now there was no one left to call Papa or Dada the way I had as a child. The word itself, *Papa,* encompassed the full measure of a childhood granted, lived and accepted. Until the end, that was what I called you; I could never see myself using your given name or the familiar *tu*, like my brothers and sisters. What sacred bond was I determined to maintain? Or what frontier was I unwilling to cross? Could it have been the hope that my childhood would one day be returned to me? By that one word: *Papa.*

It was only much later in life that I understood why I could never see you as a friend: for want of a love that was suitable to a father and daughter. Not that you were threatening, protective in fact, especially in your sixties: a good grandfather loved by his grandchildren. You suffered through years of anger, in the grip of violence, trapped by your memories of the war of 1939, the war you and your brothers enlisted in; there was no escaping the Canadian government's conscription for either you or my uncles. Despite your mixed blood, your name sounded French and your father was Québécois; in any event, you welcomed the chance to be a warrior defending your country, afterward, you carried the war inside you for the longest time, handing it down to us in the shape of constant worry, chronic insecurity: never turn your back, be wary of the ground you walk on . . . never breathe easy.

You, too, felt the distance separating us, a wound to your heart, though you never spoke of it; only occasionally would a sudden gesture or look glide over me, as soft as the down in our duvets. No one believes a baby being born understands what is underway, and yet it was at that precise moment that our love imploded, given no opportunity to know joy or the slightest growth; it shaped me, full of repressed tears and pain, yet gleeful and quite mad when I give myself over to the lifeforce bursting at my seams. You made me what I am, my mother too, of course, but this is about you, you and me. You would lean over my shoulder as I drew and exclaim in admiration. Did you understand that it was my only means of survival, my opening, however small, to the sun from which my eye never strayed night or day? Was that why you pushed me so hard to take up art, knowing that that break in the clouds heralded my hand's transmutation into the light you extinguished the day I was born? No, you couldn't have known.

So let me tell you. I was fifty already, in a relationship about to unravel like every relationship before it as soon as I'd seen what there was to see and boredom set in. Yet the man in question would help me make the connection between my life's beginnings and its sadness by recommending I see his therapist; I was tired of the struggle life had turned out to be for no apparent reason. Using a deceptively simple technique, the psychologist took me back into my distant past. With eyes closed, I felt you reject my body even as my soul arrived with its wealth of joy. I wasn't the right gender: I was a girl, a girl and a consciousness, pure incarnate consciousness, like all babies being born. No one truly realizes that, unless their spirit has been wakened. The bolt of lightning was so blinding that the child shut down; my stomach aches still, Papa, at the thought . . .

Some will say that moment was of little importance, including you, had I reproached you. My shield held high, armour encasing my entire being, I thought you would deny the truth after the words escaped my lips, "Was it a boy you wanted instead of me, Papa . . . ? When I came into the world?"

You could never lie, your expression an uncompromising show of candour, at least with me. Taken aback, you said, "Who told you? How do you know?" I didn't respond.

But none of that matters in the least, however contradictory that may sound; what I think doesn't matter since life is fate's true decider of destinies. Nothing to be said, nothing to be done, other than face squarely into the shower of stones chosen to lapidate me. And so it is for us all, every single one of us. Some have an easier time of it though, why is that?

This need to talk to you, no matter where you are or whether you still exist. To share the unbearable with you, Papa, because on this day of total annihilation, I have no one else to turn to.

A rattle accompanied his breath in and out, a harsh wheezing in his chest, his burning skin reaching frightening temperatures. The child's mother gathered together fleece-lined clothing from the baby's tiny room and called to her husband out tinkering in the garage: "Quick, start the car!"

The neighbour would come for the baby's big sister, well-behaved enough to stay home alone a few minutes while, panic-stricken, the child's parents barely took time to shrug on warm clothes. The child's mother almost slipped on the steps down from the verandah with him wedged against her.

The on-call physician at the clinic was not the doctor who had saved her child at birth two months earlier. That didn't bode well for what was to follow; the man had a reputation for carrying out only cursory exams and minimizing his patients' symptoms — in short, he was not well-liked by the locals. The nurse at the reception desk helped the child's mother undress the baby then placed a thermometer under his arm; she grimaced at the number shown. The doctor palpated the inert child, lifted his eyelids, opened his mouth and, shining a small pen light, took a quick look. His diagnosis struck, its force as brutal as a fist to the solar plexus, cutting off all breath, "There's nothing for it but to hope the fever breaks on its own, if it isn't already too late."

Winter invaded the child's mother's heart. Her hands shook as she dressed the baby. The nurse helped, muttering through clenched teeth as though in a fury, "Hurry home and bathe him in ice water . . ."

With a shattered glance, the child's mother nodded, gathered him up and ran to catch up with her husband by the exit. She resisted her sudden impulse to lay the baby naked in the snow outside the hospital. The child's father ignored every stop sign on the drive home; in this northern village, few cars were out at night. He left his wife to her task, already resigned to the fact that death would take the child it had stalked since birth, leaving nothing but a fleeting burst of light, joy amputated at its source and fear like a ball and chain around the father's ankle. In despair, he returned to his workshop, laid his head on folded arms and unleashed his anger, his grief. The child's mother filled the sink to the rim with cold

water, threw in a bag of ice from the freezer, then lifted
him from the counter where he lay motionless, touched
her lips to his forehead and submerged him in its icy
coldness. Still no response: she pushed back the terror
exploding inside her, refused to give up, reined in her
panic and the howl that had been galloping through
her chest ever since the doctor's insane pronouncement.
She spoke to her child, "You can do it, I'm here for you,
my baby . . . come on now . . . come back to me."

Her fingers could barely tolerate the freezing cold,
she had to keep switching hands to hold the baby's head
out of the water. With eyes closed, he looked to be asleep.
Again she touched her lips beneath the line of damp,
dark hair, wedged the baby against her hip, water spraying
the floor, pawed through the freezer, grabbed another bag
of ice that she threw into the sink, then immersed his
inanimate body once again.

The clock struck one. Was the dark of night about
to steal away her angel's life, along with the little time
granted for their love? She placed her mouth on his temple,
inhaled deeply without thinking, perhaps inhaling his
fever. His skin no longer consumed by fire, she enveloped
him in a towel. The soft spot on his crown pulsated gently,
rising at increasingly regular intervals; her child sighed
softly. She picked up the rectal thermometer, inserted and

removed it: 37.5 degrees . . . She clutched her son to her and, her blouse soaked from her leaking breasts, threw on a wool blanket and walked to the rocking chair, humming a tune. Scarcely burgeoning as he was, he cloaked her heart in hoarfrost. She uncovered him, wrapped her fingers around his feet, kissed the tiny seashells on his toes, basked in her child as in the setting sun. She wept quiet tears and watched over him till dawn; cutting through the wonder, an intuition was born during that long night's watch that he would be her wound, she would have to battle to keep him with her, to defend him against the worst of all enemies.

I went to see my doctor, told him about my headaches, my insomnia; he seemed upset to hear what had happened because his friend, my brother, hadn't mentioned a word. *Mon père*, death is such a hard subject to broach that sometimes people say nothing because if they opened the hatch to that raging sea of tears, how would they ever stop the deluge? He listened, told me that in my place he would have had just as many health issues, counselled me not to be alone or at least to surround myself with caring people.

"Have you done that?"

I lied, said yes for form's sake. The one friend I did confess my pain to steered the conversation around to cars, his renovation plans, and not just once, but every single time. Another wrote to say how well I was holding up, he could tell, and that we'd make time to chat one of these days. I thought of you, the way you never shared your problems; I realize it's not something your generation of men, or mine either, likes to do. But once again, that's not it; how many people I know, no matter their age, acted as though nothing had happened? I pretended to be strong, that suited them; few people really want to see. If I were to slit my wrists or throw myself into a lake, a weight tied to my ankles, wouldn't that create a problem for them! Yet I had drowned, my wrists had been slit, my heart had stopped beating; part of me was destroyed with him. No one knew. Death is an excruciating topic. The doctor diagnosed post-traumatic stress, which affected my brain and made it hard for me to sleep; I was depression-bound. He prescribed tranquilizers before bedtime. Night is solitude's sister.

I set out by car for my sister Justine's, who always welcomes me with an open heart. She was at work; on her break we went to a near-deserted restaurant for lunch. She took the time needed to gauge my state, her gaze like a laser beam tracking each hesitation, each word, each time my eyes avoided hers, her ears attuned to the silence mixed in with my laughter.

"You're not okay."

I didn't cry in front of my little sister; I was protecting her and she knew it.

I continued on the drive to Montreal, a long journey that lulled me: its departure through snow-covered landscapes and arrival to delicate flowers in my friend

Hélène's front yard. Entering the city, I drove past my son's last apartment on Saint-Denis at Jean-Talon; it hurt. I hurt. There, it's been said, it's been written. I'd begun transcribing a jumble of words onto my laptop, words that gave momentary relief from the tormented agitation haunting me.

Hélène wasn't home, she'd left for Ukraine or Romania, I couldn't remember which: she was a carrier pigeon, a world traveller, curious about lives lived elsewhere, she was also a sister of my heart, who let me use her house to rest, sleep, write ... Her house key was one of my treasures.

A walk before my evening meal preparations. The breath of air against my face like rippling water gently, almost too gently, enveloping me, its suave touch melting that already crumpling, wounded part of me. Six weeks earlier, that last meal, my last supper with my sacrificial son, took place here at Hélène's home in Outremont. His shadow remained, intact, hovering by the table, sitting in the chair that had been his. We ate salmon. My motherly offer of the metro ticket I'd kept to catch the bus to Abitibi the next morning. The two jars of pasta sauce he'd already placed in a bag. He coughed, said he'd come down with a cold. My last words were, "I love you, be careful, son."

He said, "I love you, too, don't worry!"

Outside, spring's jubilation, restaurant tables spilling onto sidewalks, bistro windows open wide to the sunlight, even the ice cream shop already serving cones in every flavour. Girls offered up their bare legs to the warm billow of the breeze's caress, trees exposed their buds in a green spray floating above my sorrowing head; my son was present, in the haunting, secret space that was now his.

The child clung to his mother's bright skirt as it dragged along the carpet, too long by a few centimetres. He loved its ground-sweeping fluidity, a red river streaming over the feet of the huge woman to-ing and fro-ing between the table and the refrigerator, delivering the milk jug, setting it down on the counter to loosen his hands from the same fabric that brushed against his face as she turned then walked away after kissing his hair. He could barely stand, falling backwards onto his thickly padded bottom; his mother's laughter, the tender joy. Immediately, he raced toward her at a crawl, a quicker means of locomotion thanks to limbs that were singularly powerful for a baby his age. "Mamma!"

He again managed to grab hold of a fold of her skirt, which he crammed into his mouth while she prepared his bottle. A melodious sound issued from the box whose button she'd just pushed and, bending down, she lifted him high in the air, then let him slide down her body and settled his tiny legs around her waist. Her arms encircling him, she twirled from the kitchen to the dining room then the living room, ever spinning, transferring the child from one hip to the other, her eyes locked on his, her lips smiling: she sang, *lala lala la la,* her long hair flying round them free, like a black waterfall, a silken, living downpour. He didn't know that the music she waltzed to was Strauss, the concordance between his mother's steps and the sound enfolding them penetrated his being like his first time in the lake: the sudden chill, a shudder, then the keen sensation of an astounding discovery and lucid, simple, pure joy.

Occasionally, she would look down and squeeze him tight, kiss his cheek, then whirl back to the other room, to the baby bottle that appeared and disappeared with each pirouette. Suddenly, the bottle nudged his lips — she had grabbed it from behind his back and pressed it up against his mouth, inviting him to take the bottle in his own tiny hands; he was no longer hungry or thirsty, lost in the bliss of the dance he thought would go on forever. He sensed silence surrounding them, his mother motionless now. She lay the child down on his blanket spread over the carpet. The explosion of joy had been so intense that his lower lip began to quiver — he cried. The skirt grazed his ear and he felt his mother's arms around him again; she rocked him and fed him his milk and he fell asleep.

I'd slept well, lying on light airy feathers, the mattress as soft and spongy as moss. I floated, drugged, on a cloud, although I couldn't drink alcohol on the medication, so I didn't use the drug every night because, I have to tell you, Papa, I liked red wine to wind down.

I was outside on the street, it was a Sunday. Sun. In my eyes. I hadn't brought sunglasses with me, my village had been overcast for so long. I made my way to the closest drugstore to buy a pair with uv-protection. Some tall fellow with an accent, an expat from France, came up from behind and reached over my shoulder, rifling through the display case; this happened to me too often, unwanted contact. A flashback: I was in Montreal visiting my son and stood waiting for the metro, it was summer, my red flowered dress was neither too short nor too revealing, nothing more than my arms left bare. I turned and felt a shiver down my spine: a man with long grey hair stared at me with the eyes of a wolf who's spotted a hare, its paw caught in a snare. I hurried off, even though, because of the crowd, I was in no danger. He followed. I slipped behind two stunning, scantily-dressed young women, trying to divert his gaze, but no; he kept coming when, all of a sudden, he stopped. I have no idea what he read in my expression. An entreaty? Rage? Exhaustion? Regardless, he stopped, reluctantly, and stepped onto the train. I stayed put on the platform, my heart pounding.

Yet I did nothing to bring it on, I didn't dress provoca-tively. In the drugstore, I wore my sister's extra-long fleece jacket and wide-legged jeans that covered my runners. I turned to stare down the fellow next to the sunglasses, but I haven't mastered a glare—I'm told I have a velvet gaze. He apologized and stepped aside, letting me choose my glasses. He walked away, leaving my gut reeling in turmoil, angry at myself for my inability to shake the frightened-victim aura I bathed in, the one that attracted predators.

In my loneliness, I'd imagine a stranger who'd become a friend, a companion, an ally, a lover above and beyond sex, one who would make love to me while his soul dove into my eyes—better yet, someone to bring warmth, his whole being. A man who would welcome my body next to his, part of his private landscape, inviting me in and I him in the glow of shared trust. A man who would see beyond the human face and reach that other, invisible face, which he would love despite all the scars, the tears, the fatigue and the despair. A love I'd never known.

On my way back, as I passed in front of a closed bookstore, I remembered I still had to read my friend Julie's latest collection of stories about the true North, the Inuit North, with its beautiful cover. Huh, I thought, your mind has turned to something other than grief, a good sign! I gave myself the occasional pat on the back to instill courage, I filled myself to bursting with the sun's light, its wan heat trumped by the cold draft born of the night. Now that I think of it, Papa, without realizing it I've been using the familiar *tu* as I speak to you, proof I have changed. The winter just past that I'd tried to escape was my first since his departure and the longest ever etched in my memory since the day of his birth. The sun deserted my land, its presence altered by dense clouds bearing sorrow and snowflakes; in speaking to you of the cold, a polar wind brushed against me and penetrated my hands.

My womb, like my life, was a gaping wound through which his winter entered.

It was a beautiful sunny day, perfect weather for errands pushing the little one in his stroller. He refused to climb in though and stayed out front, bent on walking to the heart of the village without climbing into the four-wheeled conveyance: "Me do it, Mamma!"

He came to a stop in a puddle and, without hesitation — splish, splash — he stomped his boots, laughing as sprays of water reached his mother's legs. She let him play for a while then led him away by the hand, promising candy if he was good.

The minute they stepped into the shopping centre, he made a beeline for the toy store. Fascinated by a plastic tow truck in the window, he hopped from one foot to the other and pointed, "Mamma, pretty, want that!"

She approached and swept him up in her arms, acknowledging how pretty the toy was, and steered the conversation around to the shopping to be done for the family. She pointed out a little girl nearby, happily sitting in her stroller.

"No, not me!" he cried.

She began to consider putting off the shopping trip until another time; he wanted to run free and was getting heavy so, exasperated, she set him down, "Come, I need to get you some diapers!"

She set off toward the drugstore, he followed, fussing all the while and, without taking her eyes off him, she grabbed a box from the shelf. As she slipped into line to pay, still pushing the stroller, she lost sight of her son. Busy pulling bills out of her purse, she told herself she'd catch up with him back in front of the toy tow truck, and she hurried, stuffing her purse and the diapers into the stroller and dashing out of the drugstore, but he was nowhere to be seen. Inside the toy store, she walked all the aisles, asked the cashier if she'd seen a little boy wearing blue-and-white-striped coveralls, went back out into the mall and ran from one store to the next, nothing. A surge of ice-cold panic hit her. He couldn't be outside, the doors were too heavy for him, unless someone else had let him out, but why? Anyone could see he shouldn't be on his own at his age. Unless that person had taken her child; her fear became unbearable, tears streamed down her cheeks, she made no effort to wipe them away. Just then, a young man approached, he wore a local hockey club's ball cap, had the same sky-blue eyes as her son.

The young man said, "Ma'am, are you looking for a little boy?"

She nodded frantically. "Yes, he's wearing striped overalls . . ."

The teen had come across the child alone splashing about in a puddle on the street leading to their house and, not knowing what to do with him, had simply taken the boy to the police station. She thanked him again and again, embarrassed by her tears, not knowing how else to express her gratitude and the return of joy. He gave a kind smile.

When she saw her child sitting on the station secretary's lap, his cheeks streaked with tears, his jacket striped with mucus, uninterested in her presence, busy drawing on a yellow sheet of paper, it took all she had not to drop to the ground and howl like a wounded she-wolf.

At home as a teenager, I sometimes felt so lonely
that I'd sit at the window watching for visitors who never
came. Maman was often away; I don't want to tell you
everything, Papa, just what the dreams told me, the
images they chose to reflect my life back to me. One image
is of me running to the river, fleeing an awful woman, a
witch out to hurt me. She drew near, close enough for me
to see hate contorting her face. Reaching the end of the
dock, I was trapped, either I let her catch me or I'd have to
jump into the water full of broken bulrushes and floating
feces; I gagged at the filth. I dove in and swam to where
the water was clear, it seemed to take forever, I knew
there was a small island somewhere and, eventually, it
rose out of the dark. Rocks, rigid and imposing, loomed
behind a curtain of mist. A canoe was beached there,
a paddle stored inside; I stayed on the island for the
longest time until I heard voices coming from that other
shore I'd left behind, the movement of humans I couldn't

see because day hadn't broken since my arrival. When I heard my name being called, a faint light appeared on the riverbank, I climbed into the canoe and paddled toward the strange voice. A sea of people came out of the fog, multiplying as I approached; it included my brother and sister, grown. They seemed to be waiting for someone and I turned to look as everyone scanned the cloud screen surrounding me. When I emerged at last from the mist and the boat grazed the muddy bottom, an outstretched hand helped me ashore and I realized that I was the one they'd been hoping to see.

I thought often about death, life did nothing to lift the veil of suffering it had draped over us, our family. Being the eldest, I had to take the place you two had had with the children we still were; my childhood was stolen, my adolescence even more so. Wanting to leave this world, did I venture to that other shore in search of peace and to confront solitude, true solitude, the solitude that would greet me at the end of my days once I'd agreed to drink the dark, dirty water of my life's long river?

I was so cold. I shivered despite Montreal's summer heat. My heart could no longer ferry blood to my body's extremities. His death had turned me to ice.

I curled up under the covers. Hélène had left me
the duvet comforter on her bed; her pillows surrounded
me the way my children used to in days gone by when
they'd sneak into the bedroom and slide in between their
father and me where they'd cuddle, one in front, the other
behind. My husband would get up and finish the night on
the living room couch. Soaked in sweat and their scent,
I'd keep sleeping when they left the bed to be with their
father come morning.

I lay there waiting to feel warm again, especially my
feet, then saw I'd fallen back to sleep by the clock on
the bedside table that read an hour later. Light flooded
the house. A girl in a red camisole flickered like a flame
past the window; it must be hot out for her to be dressed
so lightly.

As I walked to the park, I breathed in sun and air,
fortified by the explosion of warmth flowing over me.
A woman on a bicycle stopped to ask the way to a

neighbourhood church unknown to me; I used the address to point her in the right direction. I came across Hasidic children dressed all in black, boys whose side curls danced on their cheeks. One of them aimed a toy bow and arrow at me, ready to shoot; he was harmless but showed no respect for the person I was. He had no idea he was aiming at an Indigenous woman. If I had started ululating, what a scare he would have had. His arrow drooped, stuck in the cord of his bow; I laughed in spite of myself. The boys' fathers wore tire-shaped hats and black coats, stockings and shoes; I didn't wonder why; had my headdress been visible, they, too, given all the feathers on my body and head, would have been surprised to note I fancied myself a bird; they couldn't see the eagles perched on my shoulders. Symbols of the Great Spirit in my mother's culture, conveying our prayers to the universe.

In the park stands a concrete monument engraved with the names of soldiers from the wars of 1914 and 1939, the war you fought in. Two names struck me. John Love—imagine going off to war with a name like that—and another that seemed more appropriate, Arthur Lacroix, a nod to that mindset anchored in defeatism. To carry one's cross. You didn't raise us in the Catholic faith and for that I thank you; you believed in nothing. As an atheist, you bore your blows stoically, without complaint, like a soldier in formation during battle; we never knew what missions you were tasked with because of the blanks you refused to fill in. Blood, the dead, victories yes, but you were only at the front at the end, what did you do during those early years? A mystery. One friend told me, years after your death, that you were part of the Intelligence Service, the term you used for espionage.

I needed to give back the suppressed anger you had passed on to us, the constant fear of coming unhinged, I could take it no more: no more of never trusting a single soul.

You saw deep into people's hearts, knew their intentions, could sense each person's truth and you were never wrong; those fly-by-night men you refused to address or only spoke the strict minimum to out of common courtesy, you were right, they weren't upfront. But in each of them I looked for a part of you, you were there, both singularly present and absent, you were afraid of me, there was desire in spite of yourself; aside from Maman, I was the only female in your family, my sisters had yet to be born, you were raised among boys, you had sons; Maman could tell, she was jealous of me, couldn't help herself. The witch in my dream: I had to protect myself both from you and from her. You didn't like it when neighbour boys played with me, so they'd come calling while you were out, and when you stumbled across us lobbing rocks into the creek at the bottom of the hill, you chased them away. Your love imprisoned me, at least the sort of love you showed. And so, any man's love became so much barbed wire surrounding me.

You put your hand here, between my legs, when I was eleven, not yet menstruating. You and Maman had been drinking; my brothers and I sat with you on your bed and you talked to me about the birds and the bees, the blood that would soon flow from me and transform me into a potential mother, to be careful around boys, men, too, don't let them take me here; and your hand made its move. No one saw.

The little boy loved the clothes his older sister wore; his mother spent long hours at the sewing machine making dresses while he played at her side or watched cartoons. She gave him bits of fabric, useless scraps whose texture and variety of hues fascinated him; he fetched dolls from the bedroom and held the cotton swatches against them just as his mother did with her daughter, adjusting for size before starting to sew.

He didn't understand why he couldn't wear the same bright colours that his mother's hands fashioned into gorgeous outfits for his sister. Of course, she outfitted him too: with suits, a jacket and pants, a plain coat, striped overalls, nothing special, nothing really pretty, no ruffles, ribbons, lace, nothing flowery, nothing sparkly. One day as his mother was packing away the clothes the children had outgrown, he grabbed a dress from the pile and said, "Me want this!"

She smiled, "You're a boy, honey, boys don't wear dresses!"

He cried, "Me want, me too!"

Tears pearled below his eyelids, his blue eyes steely; his mother sighed, removed his sweater and shorts and pulled on the dress with its tiny pink-and-yellow butterflies and a bow at the back. He walked over to the freestanding mirror in his parents' room and exclaimed, "Pretty! Me pretty!"

His mother's laughter troubled him, something hurtful in her mirth; she turned him away from the mirror and, looking into his eyes, corrected him, "You're handsome, sweetheart, handsome . . . My little boy is handsome!"

He wore the dress all day and through his afternoon nap and forgot what he was wearing until his sister came home from school. Her anger: "That's my dress, take it off right now! Maman, he's wearing my dress!"

She knew the dress was too small for her, but they had a habit of bickering over every last little thing; their mother nipped the argument in the bud giving each of them a vanilla ice cream cone. Her daughter giggled, circling her brother and licking her treat, "Huh! I didn't know I had a sister, you look so funny!"

Her brother ignored her and kept his outfit on; when his father came home from work, he smiled, amused, and picked up his son just as he did every night without saying a word, only a wink to his wife. Later, after dinner,

Uncle Jean-Paul dropped by, his booming, mean-spirited voice cutting the young boy's heart to the quick; slimy contempt trickled over his body from the gaze of a man so tall the boy had to tilt his head back to see his face.

"Lookee here, you a little girl now, m'boy? Not fixin' to be a homo, are you?"

This time the child blushed; ashamed, he turned to his mother, "No more play, Mamma, dress off."

I guess we can neither foresee nor avoid the winds of malice that buffet human efforts. All the premonitions that came to me, dreams foretelling of one person's departure, another's illness, in images so exact there was no room for doubt, yet nothing connected to his death. Why such silence from my dreams? Is it because I could have prevented that death and wasn't meant to?

The year before his death, I experienced unusual aches and pains, fatigue I blamed on too much work, not enough exercise and time's wear and tear, so I spent hours out on the snowbound lake or along park trails, on skis or snowshoes, in runners or on a bicycle. The doctor ordered X-rays, but my back gave no sign of degeneration, no collapsed vertebrae. "That's rare for a woman your age," he told me.

What to do? He recommended a new mattress, a trip to the chiropractor's, told me he wasn't against alternative medicine, quite the contrary . . . the pain kept coming back, insidious, tenacious. I couldn't read the messages my body sent as it remembered the child's weight in utero, knowing that its creation — cell by cell in the moist, secret membranes of the womb, the best being chosen from his father and me to make a masterpiece — would soon disappear from this earthly plane, and lamenting that loss with every single fibre, in torment and despair.

Let's look together at your limitations that I was eager to overcome and transcend, your fears incongruous in my eyes, every single one of them. Your fear of all that was black. Not of the night, no, but of black men. It left its mark on me. That someone like you, so intelligent, so open-minded, could scorn black people. I could never understand, *mon père*. I lived for years with a husband who had four black grandchildren, my grandchildren by marriage; you never met them. Never the least bit interested, just a scornful smirk playing at the corners of your lips whenever I spoke of them.

You and I are going to play a game. When I die, I want to be at peace, relieved of the vile stains that mar your memory; I also want to return them into your hands, unbound, innocent, absolved.

Listen to what could have been.

That he would have known me without knowing me, that he would have known me before I knew him.

That his ancestors would have arrived in America
in chains while we, already here, were decimated by
the same barbarians who transported his ancestors in
shipholds from the continent unknown to me, the dark
continent as it's called. Yes, we both sang and danced,
he in his homeland, me in mine, our encounter bathed
in blood, in the most abject humanity, that of power and
the possession of one human being by another like a
beast of burden. His brothers murdered for their ideas,
for refusing to tolerate folly, my brothers for inhabiting
our territories: eradicating them like quack grass, their
presence erased, that the New World be unpopulated.
Afterward, it was easy for the others to see us as ghosts,
no more than subjects for anthropological studies,
our creations good only to be stored in ethnological
museums.

Yet we had nothing, we were naked, had no posses-
sions other than gold in the case of some of my peoples,
and a continent — he had the strength of his arms, of his
race — because we had been devastated by their smallpox
or their fire-spitting weapons; survivors grew hardened.

We no longer speak a victim's language, we cross seas,
we bring borders together, we sing a poetry of love and
sharing. His island is one of warm seas, my land is one
of cold snow; his skin is the colour of a starless night or

infused with cream tones, mine is said to be the colour of blood; on my medicine wheel and its colours, I am found to the south, he to the west; on the globe, he is from the south and I from the west. Interchangeable.

Tropical fruit would have grown on the branches of his trees; I like to imagine that he had only to reach up to grasp plenty in his hand, to open his mouth and bite into a mango, let its juice trickle from the corners of his generous lips. His southern nights, my northern sunrises, sweat glistening on his body, goosebumps on mine, nothing but differences, opposites; our paths would have crossed in the happenstance of hybrid constellations because the earth is vast. Our union would have held, it would have engraved its new words on mysteries yet to be discovered; mine would have been traced on the moccasins of First Peoples and his would have been freedom, travel, heady wine, joyous song and he would laugh his black man's laugh, crisp and booming, that would descend on me, blanketing me in the delight of warm sand; he would have been for me the word made tenderness. Then I would have understood that the path belongs to me, that the visible face of the world, my world, is mine and that it would please you and those willing to see, those who do see, those who walk with eyes open wide, those who are curious, alive, the lovers of life.

I would have reunited the lovers he and I would become, made of love a conscious decision for a tale that ends well; we would have guarded that love more precious than gold, learned to disregard differences and vexations, our quotidian embedded where the magic of history is found; perhaps we would have succeeded since dreams do exist . . . and the child would have borne the colour of scorched earth. Would you have loved him all the same? Your black grandson.

The child's Métis grandfather lived out in the country in a cabin thrown together after a first one was destroyed by flames at the end of a particularly scorching summer. The wooden building went up in plumes of smoke leaving a hole both in the bucolic countryside and in the old man's heart who, after a prolonged bender, found the courage to erect other walls around his solitude. Aesthetics being of no interest to him, from the outset his new home looked like nothing more than a shack; he never bothered to dress up the exterior, finish the floors or paint walls, no doors separated the rooms, not even the bathroom, which had only a see-through curtain to ensure privacy, so the gloomy hovel that served as the family's landmark seemed more like an animal's lair. The black tarpaper held in place by cross planks was conspicuous in its total disregard for the outside gaze.

For birthdays and celebrations, Christmas, New Year's, Easter, the child's uncles and aunts prepared copious meals washed down with wine and beer. His parents always attended the feasts; children scattered everywhere, playing, shouting, running or testing the limits of the quad or the snowmobile depending on the season.

The child woke early that day in the grey light of dawn; the stench of alcohol and cigarettes from the previous night permeated his grandfather's home. On the table sat the leftovers of forgotten desserts; he helped himself to a piece of cake that had escaped the trash bin. He knew how to go unnoticed; in silence, he explored the home's nooks and crannies, pulled his father's woolen socks onto his cold feet, made his way to the living room where his youngest uncle lay curled up on the couch, asleep under a Navajo-patterned blanket. At regular intervals, his uncle's breath lifted a brown lock of hair flopping across his face, his hand dragged on the floor; and it was as the boy's eyes followed the dangling arm to the ground that he saw a nearly untouched bottle of beer placed there by the teen before he fell into his deep sleep.

The child ventured a sip, grimacing only slightly at the bitter taste overpowered as it was by a fruity flavour, the syrupy drink sliding from his tastebuds down his throat. He hesitated for a second; "Papa and Maman might get mad . . . ," he thought, but the newfound treat was worth the risk. He took another swig, a good one this time; his legs began to tingle, his arms to prickle, his head got a pleasantly dizzy feel, a joyful effervescence came over him. He drank again and again; the bottle dropped from his suddenly limp fingers, liquid spilled under the armchair he leaned against and wet his pyjamas. Someone was up and about; the child swayed and staggered to the kitchen, where his mother, her hair uncombed, was about to bring a glass of orange juice to her lips; he laughed, clambered onto a chair then the table and, before his mother's stunned gaze, stepped to the edge and rocked back and forth before throwing himself at the floor. She let loose a strangled cry and raced toward her son, catching him just in time, "You're drunk! You stink of beer! Who did this to you?!" She was furious.

That drink, the effect it had and its taste, would never leave him.

I could hear the cogs turning, mon père, as you
wondered where all this was headed — you knew, you
can read me better now than you ever could while you
were still alive; I had lost both the man who fathered
me and the man I gave birth to, one absence behind me,
one ahead, deprived of the men in my life, the true men,
my direct relations. Of course, I still have my brothers,
but we exist on the same plane, neither forebears nor
descendants, they neither precede nor follow me along
my path, my wake, my creation; with my son's death, my
male line has been broken, severed, destroyed. The other,
the female line, is assured by precious radiant girls.

Amélie has two beautiful, luminous little daughters,
who bestow on her quiet wisdom and joy and little time
to wallow in grief. She is an enigma to me with her
capacity to accept the inevitable, her sovereign strength.
She holds her head high and perseveres, day in, day out,
with patience and grace. She and her family are my pillar,
my spine.

Yet you, my men, why were you so sombre, so drawn to darkness, the night, pain, death? So fragile? Why this lot of grief and worry surrounding you and, let's speak plainly, why did you push my suffering beyond bearable limits? A bird, one half colourful with feathers, the other dried up and grey, a broken wing hanging limp, pitiful, useless; how will I ever fly?

Where your death dug a grave beneath my feet, the death of my son digs a hole in my wholeness, cleaves my passion for life, drives me to the dark of despair. A direct hit. Until now, I managed to dodge all bullets, invisible radar warning me when to jump aside, despair unable to gain a hold; you Papa, Maman, two brothers, a sister all gone, missing because of the drama your life choices created then imposed on us. Yet the weight of those absences, those missing elements, was shared among several, that is until death deployed its remote-guided drone, confident this time in hitting the mark. Ever since, I've lived with silence ensconced in my breast and my belly where for nine months he twisted and turned, the umbilical cord winding round his neck, already headed for the inevitable. Who could understand and say, I hear you, I'm listening, other than another mother who shared the same pain? What greater mourning is there than for a child? You have known that horror. I tried, I wanted to tell

of him, of the unspeakable sorrow, words saved mostly
for other women, and for my dearest friend Marc whom
I didn't see often but whose undivided attention came
with boyish smiles, dimples in his cheeks, an undamaged
being as welcoming as a loving mother. He could never
be my lover; he felt no desire for me but enjoyed spending
time in my presence, with my inner self, not my woman's
body. Not him. To my infinite regret.

When it all got too much, a man would appear in
my dreams, a frequent visitor after the initial dream
encounter. He appeared to me a month before the first
loss, that of Henry, my eldest brother. The man was a
stranger, unknown to me yet familiar, leaning against a
cave wall, an ironic smile playing on his lips. Dreams are
like that, the choice of decor singular; his features were
dusky, their origins hard to place, perhaps many-fold,
his eyes dark. A shadow who was there for me, allowing
my words to spew forth like gravel, the vomit of loose
stones against his hands that brought peace as they
brushed against me. A church man, a space of silence and
serenity to which the wounded turn for hope and refuge.
I believed he didn't exist in real life and could only come
to me at night in my silence; I could feel him at my back,
his wholeness, and the only words he uttered, "I'll stand
behind you always."

Words woven through my sorrow despite the desert to be crossed, the thirst for eternity: those words were my lifeline, my North Star, my guide on the march when one world has ended.

In my sleep, I turned to look, to drink in his features; pure love engulfed me, absorbed by his essence I found my way home in his Christlike eyes akin to those of prayer card saints. The day I have had my fill, I hope to merge with that absolute darkness, with my luminous phantom, my double.

His presence, though incorporeal, sustained me, kept me from losing all bearings despite my appearance of waking madness. The way I saw it, given my half-crazy family, I must surely be as well.

There are those who are only on this earth in passing, not fully incarnate, who explore life as though it were a planet encountered on a journey through space. I have no idea whether reincarnation is possible; I always felt that he was of another era, long ago, and that his desire to live life intensely came from knowing how little time he had. A few years earlier, one of his aunts phoned me, she had heard on the radio the name of a young man killed in a car accident overnight; the name sounded just like my son's. Gripped in the ice of terror once more, I dialled his cellphone immediately, hoping he wasn't at work. His reaction: "It's not my time yet, Maman."

A few months after his birth, I suffered from post-partum depression after that fever that nearly stole him away; the ground split open, triggering a flurry of panic, a black bottomless pit ahead of me just below my feet, I was hallucinating and knew it, I clung to reason to keep from crying out in terror. Could it be that deep down I knew our story and how it would end? I'd stand over his crib and watch him sleep, his gentle breath on my hand calming me instantly, then I'd rock him in my arms until composure returned. In the interest of holding nothing back, that same winter, I'd let him sleep all bundled up in his sled outside as I shovelled snow. One day a neighbour forgot to cut the engine to his snowmobile and, for whatever reason, the snowmobile shot into the street and collided with our house, just a few short centimetres from where my child lay; I nearly fainted at the sight.

He and two friends built a fishing shack out of planks from scraps left over from odd jobs done by their fathers, who had helped the boys with their project that summer. Come winter, they transported the shack to the lake, installed a small stove inside and piled wood in one corner. The boys loved to go ice-fishing over the holidays. One January evening, they asked for permission to sleep on the floor in the shack; all bundled up, they would take turns stoking the fire.

Around midnight, his father, unable to sleep, checked the temperature outside, which had dropped to near-polar levels. Worried, he pulled on his winter gear and brought out the snowmobile, which sputtered then sprang to life. Biting cold seized his throat; he pulled his scarf up over his chin, lowered the visor on his helmet and, within minutes, was racing across the lake at top speed.

The full moon cast a sinister glow across the country-side, the long-limbed shadows of trees along the shore stretched like never-ending fingers toward the tiny square of the cabin from whose chimney no smoke rose. His father raised his visor, incredulous at the boys' carelessness; anguish shredded his nerves as he opened the door calling out the child's name, the wan light outlined his boy's caterpillar shape against the frost-covered floor.

His son was all alone, coiled in his sleeping bag, half-frozen, his fingers so numb he could no longer feed logs to the stove whose fire had finally died away. His father bent down, slipped his own mittens over his son's stiff hands and, in a rush of adrenaline, scooped up the boy still wrapped in his sleeping bag and sat him down in front of him on the skidoo whose engine roared, bringing warmth.

The boy's friends had given up; too tired and unable to bear the cold, they'd walked home hours earlier and forgotten to tell anyone that the child, likely annoyed at them, his mind made up to see his plan and the night through, had stayed behind alone. Having insisted, even raged, to gain his parents' consent, pride played a large part in the child's stubborn decision. He had no sense of danger, was oblivious, desperate, already close enough to the abyss to see the other side should he cross over. He was snatched back in the nick of time.

Mon père, when you placed your hand between my legs, you had no idea I hadn't been a virgin for years, at least not there, although I still was one in my mind and heart; the predator that you feared, that you kept watch for through the window, was to be found inside your walls. It was clear to me that you were as innocent as I in this matter and as trusting of the other members of your family.

I was seven the first time. He'd returned from residential school a few days earlier and we were playing in the neighbours' barn the way we used to the summer before school started; his body, over the long winter, had endured the passage of a number of clerics, the same men entrusted with watching over his childhood, preserving it from original sin. He told me about a game, a new game he'd learned there, pulled down his pants and asked me to take off my underwear, he lay down on top of me and — *mon père*, should I be ashamed? — quite simply, I had my first orgasm, it was amazing, dazzling, afterward I wanted to tell you, our parents, but he said, "No way! Papa'd kill me!"

And so I was introduced to the forbidden, a taboo had been broken, one lived out in silence in the heart of families, between fathers and daughters, or fathers and sons sometimes, often between brothers and sisters, more rarely between mothers and sons or daughters.

That summer was hot and that pleasure my last; afterward the knowledge of sin tarnished the carnal encounters between my brother and me, I no longer liked this game that was no game. He suffered from spasms that made his heart contract, we never knew the cause. You let it be, never took him to the doctor's, maybe you suspected something; my mother, panic-stricken, beat a retreat to the wood shed. That summer, I hoped he'd die from his affliction so I'd be free from his frequent demands; I no longer had a brother, or a friend, the realization didn't set in immediately, but it was there: the person who opened my body to pleasure closed off my heart in doing so. I had no idea his betrayal would affect my ability to trust men, my body responded to the act, which was normal and innocent, only the lover was neither. Your warning came too late, your awkward attempt at preserving my virginity fed into my fear of men dating back to that young girl I'd been, a fear that clung to my body and whose aroma excited and spurred males on, leaving me at times dismayed and confused. I bore the scent of a victim.

Cultures do exist in which the initiator belongs to the extended family, but not in your family's culture or my mother's, whose youth of marrying age would leave for another band in which young girls had few family ties with them; my mother told the story of how for the longest time her grandfather would hide his daughter, my grandmother, from any passing suitor.

His fingers were so frostbitten that he nearly lost
them, those same fingers that obeyed him when it came
time to coax new sounds from his guitars; the night
sheathed winter in an icy cape as thick as the distance
between the sun and the child. His parents were away
on a holiday, the children entrusted to Aunt Céline.
Not knowing how cold it would be, his mother neglected
to tell his aunt that there would be no school bus if the
school's administration decided the temperature was
too freezing to open its doors. The little boy waited and
waited at the end of the street until a neighbour called
the house to warn his aunt that he was crying and there
was no school that morning. His aunt's dismay as she
ran out half-dressed to bring him inside where she stuck
his hands under warm running water, trying to ease the
sting of his pain, and cried with him as he wailed.

When Céline died years later, when she had had
enough of suffering and made the decision to depart,

his mother called to tell her child, who lived too far to make it back in time to bid his aunt farewell. The silence at the end of the line was so impenetrable that she thought he hadn't heard, then came a cry: "NO! NO! MAMAN! NO! NOT MY AUNTIE! NO!"

A cavernous sob followed, like the belch of a pipe disgorging waste; the depth of his grief frightened her, his tears seemed unstoppable, what could she do to calm him down from so far away? He had trouble speaking through his sobs, "I loved Auntie Céline so much, oh, Maman . . . why her?"

During the pause before the tide returned to flood the line once more, his mother had a moment's inspiration. "Honey, remember, she was my sister, think of that, if you've lost your auntie then my sister, too, is dead and gone . . ."

Another long wave of silence, then these words: "I'm sorry, Maman, I was only thinking of myself. You're busy comforting me when I should be the one comforting you, forgive me, Maman . . ."

She felt again the silken touch of his love in the anguish they shared over the miles.

So the day you brought up the treasure to be guarded between my legs, your eyes burning with desire and oddly intimidated, I thought that you, too, would find your way to lying on top of me, yet you went no further. I knew your private moments. We had an outhouse back of our log cabin; one day as I sat doing my business, you appeared without warning, I could see you between the cracks in the boards. I was about to announce my presence when you stepped up to the latrine, your cock already in your hand, you'd undone your pants as you walked toward me; I was so taken aback that I said nothing. A stream of urine hit the side of the stall and sprinkled the floor at my feet, your phallus was white and huge, I would have hated to have it in me, it would, I think, have robbed my body of any capacity to climax forever; not even our innate innocence would have spared us.

A number of years after your death, I dreamt of you and Maman, we were back in the small house of my childhood and one morning on waking I pulled back the curtains over the window at the head of my bed; slender white lilies had blossomed overnight and blanketed the yard. A voice out of nowhere said, "Your father sowed those flowers for you."

I awakened, a dream within a dream, and walked into your bedroom where my mother sat crying over your lifeless body lying next to her. I scolded her, "Don't sleep with a dead man!"

I dragged your corpse to an armchair and sat it there, then went out to admire my lilies; when I came back, she had returned your body to the marriage bed and was sound asleep.

By instinct, feeling sullied since childhood, I had tried to rediscover purity by having your spirit offer me immaculate flowers.

You may have loved Maman with all your heart, but your first love left a mark on you. You kept a picture of the German woman Margot, the one you met when your regiment was sent to Berlin for the Allied victory march, with the other photos of you and your brother Jean, including the one in front of Brandenburg Gate. It's easy to imagine how your feelings linked to war's end set the violins to playing when your gaze fell on her, her round cheeks, blonde curls, velvety pink skin, and when her bright eyes pierced yours, you toppled headlong, drowning in the water of that sky blue. One day, speaking of her, you told me, "War pays no favours, it'll leave you broken inside and out . . ."

Nostalgia flooded your features; she still occupied your thoughts, that young girl who approached you because you spoke a bit of her language, and asked for more of the coffee you distributed to the starving, impoverished people. She confided, perhaps to awaken your pity, that her cousin had been raped by Russian soldiers, the first to enter conquered Berlin; it was love at first sight! You asked your superior for permission to marry her and bring her home with you; but no, Papa, so naive, that would have been collaborating with the enemy.

I slid out of bed to go to the pump for water, and the bucket, normally full for the night, was empty. Your adult pleasures came well before your parental responsibilities sometimes and the night before you had both had so much to drink that the two of you fell sprawling into bed, not that your snoring kept us from sleep. We were used to it.

I walked through the dark room, not daring to turn on the flashlight for fear of disturbing your slumber; I let you sleep so you wouldn't start drinking again. As I primed the pump, your deep voice, its timbre gentle yet husky with sensuality, rang out beside me, provoking irrational fear.

"Iche liebe sie, Fräulein . . ."

More or less meaning "I love you, Miss."

I dropped the white tin cup as you wrapped your hands around my waist. The knowledge that you were speaking to your German woman infuriated me. "Stop this craziness, Papa! I'm your daughter!"

You woke from your secret universe with a start and, realizing your mistake, embarrassed, offered me water.

If you'd been allowed to marry Margot, our story would never have been, we, none of us, would ever have been born: my children would have remained with me in the world of unrealized possibilities and we would never have known life, we would be at peace, spirits in the great nothing. The thought didn't throw me, as though I knew the fullness of nothingness; the void was preferable to this madness, this hell, this mucked-up life, the mess you chained us to with our mother, a former non-drinker. Oh! I know, Papa, I remember your words of repentance a few months before your death, your confession, "I'm the one who drove your mother to drink . . ."

You had forgotten how you stocked the shelves for parties with sweet liquor for us kids, setting the table for death, sardonic, perched on your shoulder. You introduced alcohol into your family, making of your wife an unfit mother, a drunkard incapable of seeing the consequences of her absence and her oblivion. Opening the door to abuse: she who should have protected me from you, from my brother, by being a wife to you and a mother to us all, her children. The two of you robbed me of my strength as an adult in making me shoulder too great a responsibility, much too great for my too-few years. How could I have become a well-rounded mother myself with that gaping hole as a child and a teen deprived of the right to grow up without skipping stages?

I, too, became a mother unworthy of the name, abandoning my children, worn out from all the mothering I'd had to do from the tender age of six; yes, my son's wounds, I carry them inside, I accept partial blame for his death. Such a horrific thing to acknowledge, Papa, leading inexorably to hell. Was this what you felt seeing your daughter Céline succumb to firewater, and your sons Michel, Lionel and André skirt the same abyss, only to be saved *in extremis*? When your eldest son Henry was murdered, too drunk to dodge the knife that should have struck thin air, how did you feel? How did you keep on drawing each breath? Tell me, Papa, how can I go on breathing?

He wore a white shirt and black pants. It was the first time she'd seen him dressed up, he who usually wore casual clothes, but here he was looking elegant perched on a stool. The small music group waited on stage for the end-of-year concert. On a table in front of his sister, Amélie, in her blue dress, wind instruments had the place of honour. A young man seated on a chair was literally hidden by the cello clutched between his thighs, and a small young blonde girl hugged an English horn to her chest, looking nervous. The children had invited their mother who, by that time, hadn't lived with them for several years.

She sat at a remove from the other parents in the auditorium. He struck a chord on his acoustic guitar and suddenly a flight of notes set to dancing joyfully around him. A moment's hesitation, the young people winked knowingly at each other; the blonde girl nodded and the first movement of Joaquin Rodrigo's Aranjuez concerto rose from their instruments, spilling out to the silent audience of adults. The guitar sounded and a hint of Amélie's flute, interspersed with the cello's solemnity.

As they began the adagio, the tender wave of notes blossoming under her children's hands transpierced their mother's heart. Though unpolished at times, given the level of difficulty, the young musicians surrendered heart and soul to the performance, throwing themselves into the concerto. Her son's eyes sought her out as his fingers continued to pluck the guitar strings, playing blind, and he smiled at his mother.

The phrasing grew more nimble and luminous as they advanced to the allegro in the third movement. The child missed a chord, which Amélie caught immediately; she glowered at him. He grimaced, his playing grew more assured as though navigating on calm seas; he punctuated his phrasing with sinuous jazz licks while continuing to honour the dialogue with his partners. As though improvising and loving it.

Their mother felt both consumed and exiled by her children's back and forth, detached like an island torn from the mainland by an earthquake. She should be with them playing an instrument too; alas, she had no sense of rhythm and wondered from what cosmic sphere their musicianship came since no one in the family had a talent for rhythm or sound, maybe from their Cree grandmother, who had never had an opportunity to develop her potential. She had had a beautiful voice; their mother remembered her contralto with its powerful vibrato. The children's guileless performance raised goosebumps on her skin.

Mon père, madness ran in your family; you feared your children would suffer from it, too. Bipolar disorder seems to be transmitted from one generation to the next, especially to the boys. My son was often in the manic stages of the disorder, in realms where everything seemed possible; his case wasn't as bad as others, yet that didn't stop him from seeing himself as invincible.

Your father took the train north with his family during the First World War. Abitibi was a new land that its lone red inhabitants had never sought to change, but the newcomers arrived with axes and saws to chop down forests as well as tilling implements to dig up the earth and plant gardens. Your parents built a general store next to the train tracks; your father had a good head for business and his wife, who could count and write, kept the books. To think that a century has already passed since then makes my head spin . . .

Then death toppled them, too; your mother gave
birth year after year, and when you, the fifth son, were
born, Spanish influenza had the village in its thrall.
I dug through parish registries, looking for the date of my
grandmother's death, and saw fifteen other departures
for the beyond that same month; you were three weeks
old and your family had just lost the woman who was
your father's reason for living.

I found her tomb in the cemetery and felt a blow
reading her name, engraved on the ancient white stone
riddled with cracks testifying to the ravages wrought
by the seasons. I have yet to find her nation: was she
Algonquin, Atikamecw, Abenaki, Ojibwe or even Mohawk?
All I know is that she was Métis and her mother Indian.

You never spoke of your father. The day he died, you
took the train alone without telling us, your children;
my mother knew. That's when we learned we had a never-
before-heard-of grandfather, one we would never know
now, a secret lost to the shame of madness: he had been
in an asylum for over thirty years. I asked a cousin to tell
me about him. After my grandmother died, he showed
the first signs of his break with reality: when he ordered
apples for his store, it wasn't just a few crates to feed the
small parish, but a whole wagonload. To help him out,
his customers bought the fruit and fed it to their horses,

but he crossed a line the day he walked through the village trailing his horse on a lead, the animal painted a bright red. His brother ventured a timid why. Word is his answer was, "To hide my horse from the Jerries."

The war had entered the annals of history ten years earlier.

The thing is, I quite like my grandfather's gesture, performance art before its time, the colour red heralding us all, my Cree mother, the family's artists, colours, lines, living art, art treading unbeaten paths leading out from our gut fed up with suffering, humankind's excesses and the abuse of alcohol, sex, the cold, art to rescue us from misery and from the darkness opening out onto death. As does the written word, because what I write, Papa, is everything inside me quaking with anger, helplessness, outrage. I write so as not to hate you.

We were children left to our own devices. One night, we started into town, you and Maman sound asleep after a day's worth of partying washed down with plenty of beer and the sweet wine Maman loved, making her giddy, reckless, sometimes wildly funny or stormy.

Because of a toothache, I couldn't sleep and sat up outside enduring the pain. A skunk disappeared underneath the porch where the dog slept, it barked, the skunk sprayed, the smell woke up my little brothers, but not you, not even that unbearable stench; they came outside and one said, "Why don't we go for a walk until the smell dies down?"

The air was mild, a bit humid; we covered the three kilometres to the village at a leisurely pace, aimless, no gum or chips to be bought since the stores were all closed, no one in the streets. Outside the bar, we slipped in among the few Indigenous men who tended to while away the night there; they made fun of our smell even as

they made room for us on the concrete steps and together
we watched the sun rise slowly to the east, softening the
grey of our surroundings. Charly, a toothless Algonquin
man, made a conjuring motion around my head, saying
he was a medicine man and that his power would rid me
of my pain; he laughed like a maniac, his mouth gaping,
dark and wide. My little brothers got cross at the drunks'
teasing, who called them *Tijoudji,* the nickname they
had for you, when it wasn't *Appittippi.* They said nothing
to me — I could feel the warmth of their respect for the
girl who had kept the household afloat from her youngest
years on.

When we returned home, you were both awake,
worried; Maman turned away to hide her shame because,
despite everything, she wasn't proud of your drinking
binges and my eyes full of reproach upset her. To me,
she was almost like another child since her behaviour
forced me to assume responsibility for her family during
her lengthy absences, that is, when she wasn't using me
as a shield against your — sometimes legitimate — anger.
For a number of years by that time, Maman would leave
us regularly without remorse to stay with family or
friends, claiming that now that she'd taught me how to
run a household, her work as a homemaker and mother
was done. That reasoning is common to people caught up

in an addiction and under the sway of a substance more powerful than their conscience; by lying to themselves, they're free to continue their libations without a second thought. During that whole period, Papa, you held down the fort, keeping the job with National Defense that was yours thanks to your status as a veteran.

That morning, hearing our voices, you threw open the door with a smile and said, "How about pancakes for breakfast, kids?"

My little brothers shouted, "Yay!!"

My toothache had disappeared.

His profile stood out against a sky of granite, a grey dawn, a promise of clouds with the dying of another night in the swell of morning on this Saint-Jean-Baptiste Day, a relic of ancient ceremonies paying tribute to light at its fullest, the fecundity of summer and its warmth. An outdoor show, an abundance of free beer, a friend of legal drinking age picking up the drinks for him at the service counter since volunteers stood by to check young drinkers' ID.

The site was empty, the last partiers having disappeared into the cool air of night's end.

He nodded off, leaning against a log that had been spared the huge bonfire built several metres high by the villagers, jerked his head back, with its straggling strand of hair, whenever his chin hit his chest. The screech of gulls fighting over the party-goers' leftovers pierced the silence without eclipsing the loudspeaker music that continued to inhabit him despite the fists of intoxication methodically pummeling his aching temple from within. His throat ground out clanging cymbal sounds, and his fingers tapped to a rhythm lost periodically to sleep.

His friend, Martin, stayed sober, not liking the taste of beer, and watched over the boy who, as far as he knew, had never had a drink before. He pulled some cigarette paper and a sandwich bag of weed from his jacket and rolled himself a joint; he inhaled the marijuana's acrid smoke, releasing it in short puffs that evaporated into the cool air. Worried about the boy's father's reaction, his thoughts turned to his bond with his friend, barely sixteen and already so full of sorrow, so similar to the sting of his own suffering; the stockpiling of fear, steep mountains to be scaled with only hope for crampons, the hope of avoiding a fall that could break a spine, crumple legs, reduce bones to dust, the exhaustion of misfortune, a call, a cry for an oasis of supreme tranquility, a time of calm, he knew all about it. The gaping crevasse of the future, the unknown to be crossed, the road with its many obscure, impenetrable, terrifying crossroads, barred from good fortune: together they shared the nothingness of adolescence. He threw the roach into the ruins of the bonfire, leaned toward his companion, shook him awake, "Hey, man! We've gotta get a move on, c'mon!"

He half-carried his friend draped across his shoulders, breathing loudly like a seal; with Martin's unhealthy obesity causing his legs to buckle, they advanced in fits and starts until the house came into view. The child's jeans were all muddy, his jacket spattered with vomit. He slumped to the floor in the entrance, cursing and demanding to be left alone.

I was the ship my son boarded for his journey through
life. Even so, he became a castaway since love wasn't
enough to quench his thirst for infinity, for galaxies,
stars and distant planets more beautiful than the one he
found himself on; yet he loved this planet, suffered to see
it sacrificed for our comfort, ocean bottoms dredged for
gourmet palates, air and oceans and substrata become the
dumping grounds for immeasurable waste generated by
our intentional folly. I've kept the astronomy magazines
he collected and flip through them sometimes to dream
of him, imagine him in the magma of stars buried in
the infinite.

Sidewalks jarred my bones, visions of ripping up
the asphalt and treading the earth below, so much
easier on my hips. He—an urban Aboriginal, the latest
catchword—loved the city, loved its smells, its sounds,
its forbidden pleasures; I tried to meet him on his terrain,
leaving behind my culture of vast forests, solitary lakes,

the cry of loons come September and the howl of wolves
in January. To enter his world of dust, concrete, squealing
tires, wailing sirens; not just in passing as before but
to settle there and thrum to the beat of his heart. I was
moved by the foliage of trees, apple green against the sky's
azure, a blue that reminded me of his gaze, the immensity
had now become his eyes turned on me.

What if happiness were conceivable? The pleasure of
simply being, falling headfirst into wordlust, the bountiful
tenderness of tears, holding friends' hands as they, too,
weep for lost loved ones. All love is love, even that of
tears for journeys with no return, salt for the spread like
an ocean unfurling across the table, purging my grief,
quashing the ever lurking seeds of wrath and of hatred,
its bones rattling in the winds of rage laden with despair.
Rage, so potent, so acute.

The child was no more, become a man, with a long,
lanky frame. We liked to meet in restaurants, eat and
drink beer or wine; he spoke of himself with characteristic
humour—he could be so funny. He looked at me fondly,
that I remember, such a powerful memory of his gaze on
me, so soft, so enveloping, and playfully took on a gruff
tone when in fact he was gentleness incarnate. One day,
he motioned for me to sit beside him on the grass in a park
not far from his apartment, we sat facing the setting sun;

he talked of his life, his activities outside work, his hope of finding love. He dreamed of starting a family, it was the first time I heard him speak of his desire to hold his baby in his arms. That confession brought me to tears; how could he have been a father acting as he did like an eternal child?

Mon père, I clung to those images in an attempt to convince myself I could live without him, without the moments he had granted me over the course of his inveterate adolescent's life. He was so light, so airborn, why not slide into the slipstream trailing him, let myself be aspirated by a nascent star, why not jump into the chasm of freedom he so loved? I had only to close my eyes, forget all the contingencies around the duty to live, eventualities waiting on a gesture, a well-considered choice to show the way, no more path, no more obligations, no more necessity. Not that my thoughts had turned to dying, no, but to living instead. Free. With him.

She had a good idea what her son went through once she left home, loneliness for sure. She lived in a small house in the mining town of Bourlamaque; he approached adolescence as though embarking on a war and quit confiding in her, his mother, hadn't done so, in fact, for quite some time. She owned a car, her first, and picked him up at his father's to take him home one weekend, left him the big bed and slept on an old pull-out couch with its sagging mattress. That evening, he came to her and asked in a hesitant voice if he could sleep next to her; he was already tall, taller than her, and she made room for him behind her; he turned his back and slept. In the morning, he got up late and asked for bacon and eggs.

The last time he shared his mother's bed dated back to his first and last heartbreak. She bore the wound of her son's broken heart, he who only loved once and forever an older girl he'd dated for two years: a beautiful girl, a coming together of Spain and Quebec. He'd left the region of his birth several years before, studied art, music, switched disciplines, made ends meet in and around Montreal. His mother hadn't known that the girl left him for another man. He showed up in the village his mother lived in at the time, found her with his aunties at the bar they frequented and ordered a beer. Silence incarnate, in his blue eyes a flicker she'd never seen before, he asked her to drop him off at the exit leading to his father's house, ninety kilometres away; it was winter, the holiday season. He had hitchhiked this far and was bound and determined to continue his journey through the night; he insisted.

"I'll be back in an hour, if you're still here, come to my place for the night and tomorrow I'll drive you."

He didn't budge; she went for some water to counter the effects of the wine.

The car's headlights illuminated him, a black shadow dotted by the white of falling snowflakes, the winter child among his own people; he was cold and trembled slightly.

Back in her cabin, she fed logs to the stove and heat flooded the room. He grabbed a chair and set it down next to the stove's warmth, held his hands out, took off his jacket and toque, all in silence.

"You'll have to sleep with me, I don't have another mattress," she said.

"That's fine."

In the flickering light of the kerosene lamp, his steel-blue eyes shone, the eyes she'd wished for him, a utopia, since no one else in her family bore the sky in their gaze, all of them First Nations' descendants on both his father's side and her own. When the blue stayed blue, like two azure nuggets gazing out at her, she asked around; his great-grandfathers had had those same eyes.

They'd only just stretched out on the mattress when she felt his body quiver; he shook silently, his face buried in the pillow. She laid her hand flat against his back, after all he was a man now, she had to wait, respect the space between them, he pulled away the pillow, turned onto his side and moaned, his breath caught in his chest, "Maman, she's left me. It hurts, Maman . . . it hurts so much!"

A murmur, what else could she say or do but weep with him, her forehead pressed to his, blotting their tears away with a tissue, then he rolled over and she hugged him for a moment, long enough for sleep to ferry him away. The small cabin's walls creaked under the gusts, now become a full-fledged storm, and above the bed snow tapped against the windowpane; once more, the child had escaped the cold.

For me, he had Buddhist trinkets, a cosmic egg
hand-painted in lush colours with gilt accents. From
his apartment I kept his incense burner and sticks, his
Chinese medicine balls, a little Buddha and his collection
of fragrant teas. Does the invisible reality of our soul
manifest when we die? If so, my son's soul was Samurai
with, in the days preceding his leave-taking, the same
look and complexion, his long dark hair swept up into a
topknot; for several years by then, almost devoid of facial
hair because of his Indigenous origins, he had sported a
scraggly mustache and goatee, and his eyes, while blue,
were almond-shaped. His skin, gone yellow from the
hepatitis brought on by the decline in his vital functions,
glistened with sweat; he refused to give up on life, fought
his caregivers, the doctors, us; he was at war, in a battle
to return to the street, his neighbourhood, his privacy.
They tied him to the bars of the bed, but he managed,
amazingly, to free himself, the formidable rage radiating
from my child tearing me up inside.

I managed to reassure him with gentle words and children's songs, reverting to the attentive, loving mother he had once known. He asked me to visit the island with him.

"Should I drive, or you?"

I knew he'd slipped back in time when he refused to drive, "No way, Maman, I'm not old enough!"

Playing along, I invited him to take a seat and buckle up, described the sites I knew throughout our imaginary outing, like the snack bar we stopped at where he agreed to drink the tea the nurse brought in.

My heart was ice, knowing death lurked nearby, so close, but when would it strike? When, in a sardonic rattling of bones, would dame skeleton mow him down?

Driving home after a day's shopping in La Sarre, my thoughts turned to my son, casting around for a way to force him to change his lifestyle, cut back on his binging: alcohol, marijuana, sleepless nights, gambling. I never listen to my voicemail before I've put away all the groceries and other purchases. But that day, I picked up the phone without thinking and entered the password to retrieve my messages. Heard my son-in-law, Alex, Amélie's husband, say in a strangled voice, "You've got to call Amélie on her cell. It's bad, your son's in intensive care . . ."

Silence, then a sob.

My entire being caught in a cold surge. A stab of certainty: his time had run out. Mechanically, with gestures learned in childhood in the face of dread, of fear, the need to act despite it all, I booked a seat on the next flight to Montreal. I didn't have much time. I would only make the flight if there was no traffic between home and the airport.

The habit of adversity caught up to me at full gallop, found in the stony expression separating me from the people on the plane, the crowd in Montreal, the taxi driver chauffeuring me to the hospital. Four hours had passed; I clasped Amélie to me in the corridor to the room where her brother lay dying. She told me he had contacted no one, the staff had had to insist for him to give them a family member's name, he didn't want to worry us. He meant to get through this on his own, not bother anyone, he had no idea he was dying.

My daughter took me by the hand and led me to the foot of the bed. Tactfully, his father and his father's partner stepped away. For the space of an instant, the cold wave turned glacial, flooding my heart, my womb, my breath. Dazed and trembling, I slid onto the chair offered by Amélie. When he saw me, his only words were, "Oh! You're here?"

I felt a presence behind us. The entire Montreal family stood there, silent, overcome. The child, meanwhile, was glad to have visitors.

His friend phoned; actually I called her because of an email she'd sent to tell me she'd only just found out by chance about my son's death. I could sense her distress and wanted to know her connection to him. She told me she had loved him deeply, but not he her; there were long pauses during which her words gave way to sniffling. The girl was intense, undone. I listened to her, recognizing a trait I shared with my son, the long-standing inability to love someone who would in turn love me: a brokenness. She spoke for over an hour, a great deal about herself, and about him, his refusal to seek medical help or let her advise us of his illness, his worrisome cough, his desire to vanish, to stop keeping on keeping on. Apparently, he told her, "My mother knows I'm not well."

It was his way of shifting responsibility onto me to discourage her involvement. Yet we were close, he and I, even without words, we understood each other; I'd had a vague sense that he had had enough of his life, believing himself incapable of returning to an even keel, ignoring my pleas that he consult specialists or accept help. I could see you in him, *mon père*, I could see the same look in his eyes as in my brothers' when they turned down any outside assistance, could see him mired in his pride and pigheadedness: his drinking was not a problem.

I wish he could have known happiness, I would have sacrificed a gift life has bestowed on me so far, a sense of joy, and given it to him instead; ever since his very first girlfriend, his first and last love, he had known unhappiness. The lovers he chose, either struggling felines or feral scrappers quick to unsheathe their claws: he liked strays from elsewhere, always indomitable, quick to disappear beneath the bed when visitors showed up at the door. Or friends who lived like parasites off his fridge, depriving him of food, or beer, or money.

"No big deal, there'll always be another paycheque!"

His words. After his passing, postmarked envelopes lay scattered on the table with the cheques for Greenpeace that couldn't be cashed because of his empty account once he no longer had a good head on his shoulders.

At the same time, he grew up feeling he had no right to happiness and accepted it. There had been so many trips down death's road that it became more familiar to him, more reassuring than the years stretching ahead, and he courted danger, even as an adult: riding his bike in the dark, blind drunk, down the staircase from Mount Royal, the spectacular fall that ended in nothing worse than bruises. Or skiing down the steepest slopes, poleless, his first time on skis, yet managing somehow, pushing off with a laugh, arms spread wide, hair flying in the wind, so full of life, so tall and strong that I couldn't hold him back and only my heart skipped a beat as I welcomed him afterwards. His proud, radiant smile.

I was so worn out from worrying about him that the night he finally took his leave, I slept soundly for the first time since the day before his birth. He was my moth child, flitting around the flame of the beyond; I saw him enveloped in the sheets of eternity, warm, serene at last, waiting to return, I hoped, to light my dreams. For he was still that little boy free from malice, fair and generous; his only way of being was with the absolute freedom of original purity.

The day before, I'd gone out seeking warmth; in his
bounty, grandfather Sun tugged at the tender shoots
exploding at trees' fingertips. In front of the produce
merchant's storefront, potted flowers paraded their colours
and perfumes, their delicate petals open in silky invitation;
I bought daisies with saffron hearts and oranges.

It is so hard, *mon père*, to plumb the depths of the
pool of blood that is grief. Emerging from my dive, sticky
with tears, skin cracked, the jerk of my breath translating
countless earth tremors, eyes lowered, I gently stitched the
cleansed wound back together until the next time. It had to
be done, for life's sake, so the path wouldn't end, the path
of poetry in all things, the whiteness of canvas waiting for
paint, the smiles bestowed on those left behind.

I didn't like the way the doctor's sedatives scrubbed
at my thoughts, mired my brain in gelatin, imprisoning
words, turning sentences into snails, slithering trails along
leaves. The pills wound me tight in plastic wrap, crushed

the nimbleness of prose, my body had no tolerance
for chemicals, my insides liquefied; in the end, I chose
sleepless nights over the half-light of impotence with
drool hanging from my lower lip.

Daffodil blossoms fired golden sparks across the
tender green shoots of the lawn. I had not yet found the
courage to revisit the various apartments my son had
occupied over his twenty years in the city, a pilgrimage
so as to be with him, keep him here with me a little
longer. I knew each of his abodes. But I could no longer
remember the address of the apartment in the west
that he had shared with other students. I had visited
him there once. He started washing plates to serve
up the pizza I brought, the counter invisible under all
the dirty dishes, his friends partying on, leaving it to
him to pick up, clean up. He had decided not to oblige
anymore, so the mess had grown; he was set to move to
an apartment by Café Cherrier, a grim dwelling invaded
by cockroaches as soon as the lights went out, where he
slept with his bedside lamp on.

He was playing the blues on his guitar. It was summer;
the two of them had planned a get-together for her birthday,
for a meal he himself would cook. The door had been left
ajar and she stood behind it for the longest time, listening,
losing herself in the notes; she hadn't knocked because
the music was so beautiful, solemn, sensual and profound,
thick with alluvial tones. Enthralled by the movement of
his fingers over the strings, she slid next to him to watch
him play, his torso bare, his wet hair cascading over his
face, his back, his chest. It was as though he didn't see
her, caught in the spell of the magic streaming from his
instrument through the loft. She had no idea where his
imagination had transported him right then, but could see
beneath lowered lids the dull blue-green waters of a bayou
in which giant mangrove roots plunged, teeming with
crustaceans, strange fish, even impassive alligators whose
bellies were full, then on slender branches floating on a
sea of sky, birds of blindingly luxuriant colours squawking

loudly enough to rupture eardrums. There was a scent as well, liquid and sweet, of flowers, of faintly putrid ponds lying immobile under a blazing sun and of sleeping breezes that no longer blew.

His guitar sounded a strident note like the hiss of a snake darting into thin air for no reason other than to gauge the force of its thrust, then he reined it in so skilfully that it seemed not false but calculated, in such a way that no other note could have filled the breach in his mesmerizing instrumental. He returned to a gentler, more ethereal shore, with delicate strokes like white ibis tracks on the sand, barely visible, instantly erased by the swell of a shimmering sea on a fine summer's day.

When she opened her eyes again, his steel-blue gaze, glowing with pride, took in her delighted expression; he finished with one last long drawn-out flourish that faded under his fingers to the flow of a warm, fragrant river and said, "*Song of the Bayou for My Mother:* that's my gift to you, happy birthday, Maman!"

That February, day broke with a crystalline light,
the blue of stained glass on the eastern front. The family
had invited me on a snowshoe outing followed by a meal;
my brothers and sisters were happy to see me smiling,
trusting that grief's next chapter would be smooth.
They had no way of knowing though that the joy they
saw on my face came from my secret decision to leave
them all on the summer solstice, that was the prospect
that cheered me; I'd chosen the moment based on projects
I still wanted to complete, all my papers in order with
the lawyer. My leave-taking wouldn't be a spontaneous,
desperate gesture, but well-thought-out, at least that's
what I tried to tell myself, overwhelmed and angry
at how life had taken so many of my loved ones away.
The fact dame skeleton had gone so far as to attack my
womb was the worst of all; convinced she wouldn't stop
there, I was ready to offer her the sacrifice of my own
life's breath.

My brothers walked ahead, breaking trail through
the thick snow, trading places as each one tired.
Emanating from them was the beauty of men who had
travelled down dangerous paths along which voluptuous
sirens beckoned, yet here they were accompanied by
their womenfolk, strong and loyal, thirty years or more
of sharing a bed, bliss, tragedy, laughter and tears.
Despite it all, I could still hear them conjugating their
love in the present, taking their partners by the hand to
drink the clear water of the sky with wide-open eyes and
devour the wind with abandon, steadfast companions.
They had prepared many dishes, various salads, pasta
topped with a perfect sauce, a light dessert, their love of
cooking inherited from you; they were heartwarming
with their colourful aprons and the wooden utensils they
handled like weapons, sword-fighting around the kitchen
counter, anything to make us laugh.

How strange, *mon père*, that you passed on your
sense of coupledom to your sons but not your daughters.
I imagine daughters inherit theirs from their mother,
from her example; ours had been bitten by the nomadic
bug. There were four of us girls and not one of us had
inspired in any man of the moment the light that shone
in my brothers' eyes when they gazed on the women in
their lives.

She and Amélie had just bedded down for the night at Hélène's house when his father phoned. The two women had spent the day at his bedside; a simple change of position to smooth out the sheets beneath him turned out to be enough to stop the beating of his heart. Already that afternoon, the doctor had warned them there was no hope left, or so little. She clung to his *so little.* The doctor mistook her for the child's partner or older sister.

"No, I'm his mother . . ."

She saw pity in his eyes, and the long years during which she, amputated, would be obliged to endure life without him.

"I'm so sorry, Madame . . . so sorry."

Untreated, his pneumonia had deprived his heart of oxygen and, to compensate, his heart had enlarged to the size of a bull's.

Slowly, they put their clothes back on and called a cab to take them to the hospital. On the way there, her

daughter leaning against her, his mother tried to envision
the transition from her living son to the corpse she would
gather into her arms, an ordeal so great as to double her
over, arms wrapped around her belly. The pain was such
she had to cling to the bars of his bed to keep from falling,
from blacking out; she could feel the roots of her hair
stand on end, icy drops of perspiration rolling from her
scalp along her neck. Despair inhabited her, her thoughts
wild horses throwing themselves against barbed wire in
the dark of night, she wondered if her own heart were
not about to explode, it could happen at any moment;
the pain on which she tottered was so intense it took her
breath away, she slumped on the crest of a wave about to
collapse, implode and ferry her to bottomless depths. She
spiralled into a space where nothing and no one existed,
spun there in the void, embedded in the unbearable, a
living, breathing wound. It was then that she looked on
his face, grown younger. His delicate features in their
frame of long hair underwent a transformation as though
in slow-motion, growing serene, the few lines of age fading
from his flesh as though he had gently drifted off to sleep.
She started to breathe again.

She could not conceive of leaving her son's body;
how did other mothers manage to break away from this
torment, this wrenching of the heart? She brushed his

hair, cut a few locks for herself and her daughter, braided the rest, pulled back the sheet and drank in the warm hue of his still-living skin, the slenderness of his hips, the firmness of his legs and shoulders. She gathered him to her, wiped the sweat from his back, kissed his cheeks, his nose, his forehead; breathed in his vinegary scent.

Amélie said, "He looks the image of Christ, don't you think?"

She was right: he the sacrificial victim so that, in his memory, other family members might stop drinking.

Later, in the arms of her friend Marc, far from her daughter, a bestial howl escaped her lips, or more like one final cry before the agony of dying, which itself is silent and from which there is no return, its presence borne against our will, overriding the instinct to survive, as we realize the worst always comes to pass, eclipsing rash hope, the quest for new horizons or the endless pursuit of a love to come hoped to be immortal, the possible become impossible. When death is all there is, victorious, the regent of day and night and of the world, death alone, implacable, absolute.

She collapsed against him, her unending cry dismaying in its shamelessness; she fell to her knees, he too crouched, wrapped arms around her, hugged her so tight she couldn't breathe. His sobs mingling with hers, his moans matching hers and his words, "Stop . . . you're hurting me, you're scaring me . . . please!"

She stood and hit his chest open-handed, "But I'm hurting! I've never hurt so much! Do you hear? Never, ever, ever . . ."

Her voice trickled off in her friend's damp shirt, she kept crying, sniffling, a trail left on its cloth; for the longest time he rocked her, his tears falling on her unkempt hair.

Go through the motions, step into the shower, pick up the shampoo, pour it over head, both hands massaging in a soapy caress, the pleasure, despite it all, of hot water gliding over her breasts, her belly, then doubled over with the weight of a memory of the child floating in her inner ocean like a miniature seahorse tied to the earth by a cord of flesh. She flung herself against the walls of the wet stall and collapsed, felled by the powerlessness of her rage, limp as a jellyfish washed up on the sand.

The family decided on cremation without a wake. Amélie returned to her daughters and spouse; it fell to his mother to pick up the ashes at the funeral home, thankful for her friend Marc, so loyal and attentive he accompanied her all the way back to Abitibi. With the funeral urn on her lap, the air between them grew heavy. She knew her sobs cut him to the quick, but he waited for calm to be restored before speaking.

Her brother Paul and his wife met them at the door without a word, the others waited inside, reverent, silent. They had prepared an altar with a picture of the child surrounded by bouquets of flowers. She placed the urn among the flowers. Her family showered her with love, a tender, comforting interlude. The day passed as one after another told stories of the deceased, punctuated with laughter and tears. They were readying themselves for a sacred farewell ceremony in traditional Indigenous fashion. Being the eldest, his mother would be the one to preside over the ritual to return the dust of her son's remains to Mother Earth. As soon as Amélie and her family arrived the next day, the procession began to the cemetery a kilometre away.

Lionel brought a shovel and dug a hole in front of the headstone engraved with the names of their parents, their brother Henry, their sister Céline. The group formed a circle, the child's mother beat the drum, a low, booming note, and her clear voice climbed skyward in a chant as tender as it was heartbreaking while the members of her family, each in turn, raised the urn to each of the four directions and prayed softly. Then his mother emptied its contents into the hollow, entrusting his mortal remains to the loved ones sleeping there, offering an entreaty for peace for her son's soul. Each person came forward to place a handful of earth onto the burial ground and returned to his or her spot in the circle. Peace settled over the group — the ceremony bringing acceptance of death — now left to live through the period of mourning and absence.

A bird flew through the car window, only averting death thanks to the opening that kept it from smashing its skull. I stopped to roll down all the windows, raise the hatchback and free the bird; farther along, an otter ran across the road just under the car. I slammed on the brakes; the otter too, its underwater undulations a symbol of absolute femininity and sensuality, continued to live. Signs, messages linked to the forces of the invisible.

I was on my way back to the big city when the bird and the otter taught me I would survive; I continued to visit my son's favourite sites, always setting out from my haven in my friend Hélène's home. I was reading *Folle* by Nelly Arcan who was anything but crazy; depressed, perhaps, but not mad. One passage stayed with me in which she spoke of her abortion, the heart-rending choice she had to make; I couldn't help but wonder why life sometimes puts us in unlikely situations at unexpected times. To provide another avenue? Or the certainty of doing the right thing? Of making the right choice?

Before the child, an earlier pregnancy had gone wrong at around the three-month mark, the fetus deserted my body for no reason; cramps in the middle of the night and that morning the fetus fell into the toilet bowl, a small white shrimp-like shape dropping down, and I pushed the handle. Without thinking. Flushed the toilet.

It took a long time for life to adhere to my womb again. This time, unlike my other pregnancies, I suffered from morning sickness, the child announcing his arrival. When he was ten or so, I told him about that other experience. I hadn't thought it through, and so was struck by his unexpected and pained reaction. He blanched, "Maman, if your baby had lived, I wouldn't be here? Did I take that baby's place, Maman?"

I can hardly bear the memory because he was right, his father hadn't wanted any more children after him; I stammered out a reply, all the while knowing that a wound had been opened deep in his fragile sensibility, his piercing gaze announcing he was an imposter, yet no one could ever have replaced him, my son of light, but there was no convincing him otherwise. Now though, I think he knows.

Italy came to her in the shape of a friend, Gabriella, with her tales of dreams, islands, cuisine, art. The country had beckoned to her on several occasions, through artists with whom she exchanged letters in those pre-email days. Each exchange ended in silence when she stopped responding to invitations after several visits, not that she hadn't enjoyed the Italians, their way of seeing a woman's unique cachet, her fire; she had seen works by the great masters, Botticelli's *Primavera*, Michelangelo's too-perfect *David,* the sensuality of its lines and shapes; she had visited the rocky hilltop of Assisi and communed with St. Francis' energy, palpable and deeply moving, whatever one's beliefs, once mental barriers were let down.

This time, it was for Gabriella that she agreed to one day travel to the heart and soul of Italy, Gabriella, whose daughter had quit eating, food become her enemy, Gabriella, who feared death awaited her daughter. Their words intermingled, red-suffused words issued from rent motherhood, coloured with helplessness and stubborn hope, tear-soaked evenings that flew by all the same since she was no longer alone speaking of the same sorrow, the intrinsic vulnerability, its essence painful and pure, of those who bear the world's children. That day in early May, as they strolled through Montreal's botanical garden, she invited Gabriella to go with her to Abitibi.

She told Gabriella her dream of an encounter on the twelfth floor of a building, in suite 1212, an empty room save for a desk at the back behind which a man in a jacket and tie waited, fingers interlaced, the desk bare of files, paper, pens. On the wall behind his head hung a safe from which a gentle golden light emanated. The man told her the safe held the store of happiness reserved for her.

"I'm not ready, there's so much work I have to do . . ."

He answered, "No matter, it's yours, it will wait for you, come back whenever you like."

At the time, the dream troubled her, unaware that death would soon visit her family, and she grew to see it as a sort of talisman hidden in her memory, a tenuous link to the hope that, in passing, the years would bring her isolated moments of serenity as did colours on paper. The dream came shortly before the knife to her brother's chest, her mother's ruptured liver and her departure nine months after her son, a pregnancy's span, her sister's drowning in firewater and her father's silent leave-taking. And now, the disappearance of her child.

Gabriella told of her Sardinia bathed in sunshine.

"You'll see, there's a secret place, an enclave among rocks, where the sea rests from the roar of its waves, a small beach of white sand, you'll love it, we'll swim there, in the hush, far from the din of human beings."

She'd also say, "Enough of the cold, winter, death! Open the door to happiness, open your heart, despite death, in defiance of death ... come, my friend."

The rising sun cradled the flight of the eagle's feather,
its light caught in the deep lake of the feather's eye;
she had returned for a while to the wilderness of her
lands, what words to express how, if she ripped away the
arrow planted in her womb, the last of her blood would
drain away?

It was the day before Mother's Day, so painful, so
sorrowful, too much to bear; snowing, of course, in May,
there would be no phone call with his sleepy voice on
the other end, "Happy Mom's Day, Maman!"

Talons ripped through the place his body had rested,
where his weight had lain heavy and his feet and fists
had struck the living walls. Every night since his death,
she spoke his name haltingly, half-asleep, a call, a plea.
Then one night, a dazzling light shone in the confines of
her room; he was there, took his mother into his arms,
his embrace bathing her in a love so absolute she could
barely breathe. There with him, she gave herself over to

the liquid perfume of perfect joy; a feeling she had never before experienced that met every expectation, she clung to him, tried to pull him closer, into the shadows. He pushed her away tenderly, said, "No, Maman, my place is no longer here. But you, go, all will be well, you'll see."

A dream so real she groped blindly, felt the sheets with her fingertips. The wind raged outside, blasting snow against the windowpane, an accomplice to the sudden winter that accompanied his nocturnal visit; she rose and caught sight of her face in the mirror, two new worry lines below each eye, channels running along her nose to catch invisible tears, furrows within which he buried himself, hidden from sight. And so he returned her life to her, the assurance that he lived on elsewhere, in a state of bliss beyond the grasp of the human mind.

Her Italian friend came with her to Abitibi. She let Gabriella soothe her, listened to her, shared in the bubbles of laughter that burst through the tears, a fast-moving river flowing over their secrets. They let the waters guide them, motionless, waiting to see what lay around the next bend, and held onto each other, soul sisters, their anguish transformed into a spring lapping against their banks. On a day when the sun shone and a warm breeze dried perspiration as it formed, easing the heat's intensity, they drove down the dusty road that led to Nepawa Island.

Gabriella was fascinated by the covered bridge, there were none in her Sardinia; on the long dock jutting into Abitibi Lake, they spread out a blanket on which they set down a picnic basket.

"I'm going in . . ."

Gabriella waded through the icy water; a muskrat swimming in her direction brushed up against her: a surprised cry and the small creature disappeared only to resurface closer to shore. She proclaimed the water magic with its silken touch that enveloped her in its calming essence, guiding her into its tranquil depths.

Closer to the horizon, a maze of ice interlocked, cracked and crashed, its walls warmed by the sun; in the distance, two birds frolicked in the blue of the sky, too far off to be identified. The pair flew, cartwheeled around each other, a lustful dance if ever there was one, then, in one dive, in profile, the sleeker of the two was seen to be a bald eagle. Their dance brought them directly overhead where they waltzed for a short while, long enough to inspire Gabriella to cry, "Oh, my God!"

Gabriella threw herself at her friend, her face radiant, and exclaimed, "It's just so beautiful! Thank you, thank you, thank you!"

"But I had nothing to do with it!"

Their laughter rang out across the lake.

She hoped her friend would return to Sardinia full
of Abitibi's colours and fragrances. Gabriella. Whose
hands released cool energy as she massaged away the
pain in her lower back, the pain that fractured her nights
into bouts of sleeplessness. Who massaged her scalp and
eased her migraines; who found it hard to believe when
she thanked her for her magic healing touch.

At long last, the sun made a days-long appearance,
hot and bountiful from sunrise to sunset; summer's
solstice approached, its light more lasting, gaining on the
dark. They pulled on hiking boots to climb Aiguebelle's
hills on the very day the park opened, its name taken
from those same pre-Cambrian hills. The surface rock
formations date back not millions but billions of
years and are among the oldest on earth. At one point,
the waters separate, heading either north or south,
giving the very territory its name, *Abitibi* or watershed.
A sacred name.

Her legs felt heavy as they climbed, lead seemed to flow from the rock and cling to her body, rooting it to the ground; a squirrel sat on her foot to nibble on a pine cone. Standing before the precipice overlooking the lake hemmed in by two rock walls and straddled by a steel-cable bridge ending in an odd sculpture of a giant bear, Gabriella could feel the power through the soles of her boots; she took fright and tried to cry out, but her throat seized up and she gave nothing more than a squawk. Her friend slapped Gabriella's back so she could take her next breath. A blue butterfly flitted about her face and landed on her cheek, a long, gentle kiss while its wings beat softly. Since she was poised to bite into an apple, the butterfly flew to her thigh, where it continued to fan its wings open and shut to the beat of her pulse. An eagle screeched and wheeled overhead. Filled with wonder, Gabriella burst into her childlike laugh.

life

A woman in me

suffers immeasurable pain.

And yet my flowers, my love

and my affection blossom still.

JEANNE-MANCE DELISLE

I still have so much sorrow, it's as though I will
never be comforted, my son, ever . . . yet I feel you here.
I can't help but smile despite my anguish, which comes
and goes, retreats at times when I remember that you no
longer suffer, that you exist like a star, distant but real
and radiant or like the unseen breeze caressing my cheek.

Cry with me, lean your sky against my forehead,
gather the angels around us. Tell me that the earth is
beautiful, that the horizon has a place for me. Your
phantom fingers float over the strings of your soundless
guitar; tell me I owe it to myself to live and that all music
hasn't died with you.

I am a lustrelost woman who hides behind her
autumnal beauty, her abundant leaves dying with the
seasons' suns, her foliage quivering still in the winds of
life, all for the memory of splendour to be shared with
you when winter has passed and I reach the end of the
path lined with stones that wound my feet. At times,

the ground becomes brittle, thins into November's frozen sheet of water. I have turned to ice, all day long fishermen drill their holes in me, freeing bubbling springs of hurt; tell me, does ice suffer when pierced? The quicksand of sleep, a gentle slipping away, silken, murky danger; crusty eyelids, the queasiness of unfulfilled stupour as night falls, no assurance of a return to daylight; I sleep the way others raise the mind-numbing bottle or inhale the white powder that unfurls spirits' wings. Mine fold behind the same desire for annihilation felt by those who drown themselves or set themselves on fire; solitude stretches across my pillow, imbued with sadness, yes, but at least it won't leave me, it will honour its promises.

Today the day attached itself to the top of a fir tree with clouds for wings like an angel atop a Christmas tree; my footsteps led to the forest, I looked for myself in vain. I have not heard from you for many weeks, yet silence ferries each of your words, my son, their power standing tall next to trees, tender on fresh moss and as sharp as ice at spring breakup. Word lies on its side and offers itself to latecomers, poets and dreamers borne on a love for all that stirs and goes silent; it hisses like a furious snake, cracks like a rock sundered by cold, rumbles with the earth's entrails, punctures the heavens like a supersonic plane and chants the song of lovelorn whales.

Never will the imprint of your moccasins be erased from glistening snow or spring's muddy paths.

I sought spells by magicians, medicine women keepers of occult incantations to deflect misfortune and its icy grip. They say fruit irrigates the blood, that fruit's pulp destroys the traces of unworthy visitors, nocturnal strangers who bare their teeth and clutch at our sheets revealing stiff arms of bone. And yet fairies had placed a horn of plenty at the foot of your cradle.

You thought your stamp as an artist was nothing, could never be in vogue or worthy of framing. What nonsense! Just look at the ultramarine existence of your inner seas, silent, camouflaged by the flamboyant strokes you destroyed. You hesitated, pigment dripping down the canvas, unable to see the country taking shape like a luminous spectre under the trace of your palette knife: behind mountains, flat burnt sienna amassed above the delicate thread of your lifeline. The beauty of the world was yours for the taking, pulsing in your tubes of colour, extending beneath the fibres of your brush and obeying the magic of your gestures; nothing you made was counterfeit. I recognized the occasional flash of pain in your eyes when you thought I'd dozed off unmindful of your presence; one day, perhaps you would have gone beyond the barbed wire that tore at your skin — planted by your fears long ago—to silence fear, protect the child from his loneliness, his sorrow, open the dam to your belly, let all your voices triumph over confinement and you would live still, your children would dance, joy lodged in their retina like an arrow, look too at their heart beating under the fabric of hope, it's they who would drive away dame skeleton.

If I told you that my own magic is born of terror, of the flight toward an always-elusive day, from the black line to the white line, that I keep watch along the horizon's curve, a butterfly on the firing line, I long for sleep, for the wild bird clamour of my thoughts to die down and recede into oblivion forever. I wait for you to return in my dreams.

But the storm is rising, so I set down on the table a fragrant cup of coffee and the keyboard beckons my fingers. I can feel your presence when cold creeps in, when snow dusts my window; I can no longer see the shadows at the edge of the forest, nor the salt and pepper of birch and aspen trunks on the ptarmigans' mound.

The gloom erases the ash-blond silhouettes of spruce on the hill across the way, the roar of wind slices through the silence of dawn; I am snug, in the warmth of well-being, in a moment of truce, worries lulled, nestled close to the comforting purr of the wood stove in the face of winter; my love is of the utmost rigour, like your mutation

into a snowflake spirit tumbling against the frosted pane
that blurs the outline of the world beyond, one I sense
bent on going about its business, its work on behalf of
the universe flinging human beings about in a magma
of blood and nameless viscera. The house creaks and
complains at the contortions of its frame, nails explode
in muffled bursts.

Often strength fails me, unravels and a veil of
sadness drops, either to be rolled into a wad or left to be
torn to shreds by the violent gusts ridden by the spirit
of the taiga's manitous. From dawn to dusk, the day's
tasks obscure the shadows looming over me, the scythe's
silhouette concealed inside, they calm the convulsions of
my hand gripped with panic and repulsion at the thought
of larvae crawling over my corpse, penetrating my nostrils,
exiting through my eyes.

Your breath stays with the Bear clan, the clan of our
joys and sorrows. I remember the simplicity of days spent
in the warmth of tents or makeshift shelters during treks
in search of geese or antlered creatures; the pursuit of
dreams has little of the thrill of the hunt we left behind
in the sparse woods of our past.

The life you never knew.

But mornings return, nights recede breathing deep of
the world's plenitude, my love, you departed triumphant

to meet the Northern Spirit, toward the path of our ancestors, those who carried life's burden in stone tools and robes of hide; to what trembling will my heart be invited during the dance of uncertainty? Anguish tugs at my sleeve and draws my gaze to the light of stars ablaze in the infinity of nocturnal space, where you now dwell.

I borrow the words of a beloved poet to say to you that your peace settles on me like snow.

Among the Oglala Lakota people, traditional purifi-
cation practices entail four days of intense, rigorous trials
during which participants fast and drink very little.
After Gabriella returned to Italy, another friend invited
the child's mother along to Dakota for her sixteenth and
final initiation rite; she would serve as her friend's moral
support and assistant during the demanding spiritual
ritual. There are moments in life that arrive wholly
unannounced, free of expectations or demands, paths
that open onto the unknown with utter unpredictability.
Anouk, her Innu friend, told her, "I'm not sure why, but
you have to come with me to the land of the Sioux. Many
Innu and other Québécois take part in the ceremonies."

She had always wanted to see the site of Wounded
Knee, the Black Hills, the Badlands and the likeness of
Crazy Horse carved into the mountain. She had planned
to travel there with her son someday, acquaint him with
landscapes and peoples other than those found in his part

of the world, maybe lead him as far as Arizona to participate in First Nations' healing ceremonies, telling herself
it might be a salutary shock to his system that would free
him from his addiction. They never got the chance to go.

During the road trip, eagles soared overhead; she
knew her friend was a great mystic but hadn't realized
to what extent. Anouk shared a picture of her twenty-
year-old self: mini-skirt, a tattered blouse, high-heeled
thigh-high boots, visibly drunk. At the first Sioux hamlet,
the destitution on display along its potholed sidewalks,
unpaved roads and dilapidated homes distressed her
deeply, similar to the First Nations' villages in her home
region of Abitibi. Soldiers back from Iraq, mutilated,
encased in wheelchairs — the only luxury item in sight,
a gift from their country — begged while clutching a
bottle of beer.

The sun was so hot she felt dizzy when she had to
leave the air-conditioned car. They would camp on site.
She had serious misgivings about staying in this scorching, treeless territory. South Dakota verges on immense
plains, such a contrast to her land of woods and lakes.
She hadn't been able to bring herself to participate in
the same grueling ceremonies as her friend — she felt too
fragile and far from physically strong enough — so she
didn't know why she had come.

Cool, pleasant nights tempered the days' heat; their hosts had erected plank roofing under which the guests watched the dancers, in near total comfort.

The next day, she helped Anouk prepare her initiation regalia, a long flowered calico dress and red fabric wristbands adorned with wild sage picked on site; she was told to be careful when she ventured onto the plain because its wild grasses hid rattlesnakes. She and her friend ate together that evening for the last time: from then on Anouk would sleep in the teepee with the other dancers who, with rhythmic steps, would circle the sacred tree under the brutal sun for the next four days and, on the last day, undergo the sacrificial scarring. Anouk told her, "You might find it hard to watch us, but remember that, for me, drinking myself into oblivion was much worse!"

At the break of dawn, though exhausted, she obeyed the sudden clamour ringing through the camp and crawled to the tent opening. The Nakota language, a clash of guttural, abstract, foreign-to-her-ears words, reverberated in the clear morning air, pierced by the rallying cries of booming voices. The men formed a double row, down which the women entered the sacred space in their beaded dresses, each forehead bound by a leather band, advancing slowly, with small chiming steps thanks to the bells they wore around their ankles. As the deep drumbeat sounded in the raw light of the rising sun, it was the warriors' turn to rush to the centre and execute a frenzied sarabande inside the circle of the women's round dance. They were stripped to the waist, their torsos and faces painted, their cries ricocheting off the walls of already sweltering air, their hair, either loose or braided, bouncing on backs glistening with sweat. Loincloths were festooned with red, blue and yellow ribbons decorated with silver tin cones colliding against each other: a discordant tumult, a drum roll, the sound of the dancers' bells in the two-step, the drummers and their rasping chants. Her pulse raced and thumped as certainty like a gong rang in her chest. Instinctively, she knew: she was where she was meant to be. She breathed in the animality of the dancers' frenzied whirling mixed with the smell of hot sand, admired the fierce vitality and wild determination of the Sioux, their brown flesh streaming with sweat, streaked black from the dust they raised as they tumbled and spun.

And so it would continue for four days.

A strange phenomenon intrigued her.

Alone in her tent each day, she rose at dawn when the warriors' greeting to the sun rang out: *OKKA!* The guests gathered around a space set apart by short red and blue sticks where a man handed a sprig of sage to four people chosen at random, who then became the bearers of the ritual pipe, which they presented to the participants gathered in a circle. She was chosen every single day, and yet there were at least two hundred other candidates for the millennia-old ritual. She waited patiently for the gift she felt Anouk had promised her, the one to come from her time among the Sioux.

On the last day, the heat eased thanks to a wind announcing a coming storm, and she decided to acquire a memento on her own flesh of her stay among this open-hearted, generous people, so resolute in the spirit of sacrifice. Large eagles rode the raging winds overhead whose force had yet to make itself felt on the ground.

She stepped into the long line of people waiting for a notch to be cut just below their shoulder. Word was that actual physicians were the ones making the incisions, she told herself it couldn't be any worse than a vaccination.

She spotted him from a distance and wondered whether she wasn't dreaming, he was so strangely familiar with the woolly hair he wore in a long braid, his regular features set off by the slight crook of his nose, his matching lips; he made a quick incision into each volunteer's flesh and an assistant handed him clean scalpels, placing the used ones in a wicker basket. When her turn came, he hesitated for a moment, his gloved hand encircling her arm. He looked at her, a question in his eyes; she felt flushed or maybe very pale, near terror-stricken, a moment of total confusion, then, without hesitation, he carved four bleeding furrows into her skin. He was left-handed.

She felt nothing. Neither on her flesh or deep inside. Transfixed.

It was he, the church man.

She felt outside time and place and desperate
to talk to Anouk, but her friend had to spend one last
night in the teepee sharing her first food and drink
with the other female dancers. Violent squalls laid the
tents almost flat, the days of ceremony were drawing
to a close and to the west, where the final sunset shone
blood-red, terrifying clouds swarmed the skies streaked
with lightning. From inside their shelters, the warriors
sounded the rallying cry and drums echoed once more,
making her heart beat even faster. The male dancers
were magnificent; barely clothed, they threw themselves
into the sacred circle, breaking into full-throated guttural
song. Once again, their feet stomped the earth in a wild
round dance. After several minutes, the gusts changed
direction, returned to the east, forcing the sombre cloud
masses to skirt the site. The amazed campers couldn't
believe their eyes and gave thunderous applause to
the Sioux's nature-attuned performance. She laughed

in astonishment, dazzled by the phenomenon, and ran to a hill to witness the imposing spectacle: on one side, a sky glowing pink and orange from the last rays of the sun, on the other, the sombre storm clouds, still illuminated by the flash of multiple, ephemeral arrows, and between the two a round opaque moon, the promise of a clear night. She turned back toward the camp and gave a start: the physician, the church man, stood nearby and had been standing there for she didn't know how long, contemplating the same scene in silence. Behind him, the teepees and tents had stopped shaking, people had lit fires and stars shone in the eastern sky from which gentler breezes carried the perfume of sage and sweetgrass. His voice with its metallic rasp cut through her like a knife, sending a shiver down her spine.

"But you speak French?" she asked, just as he said, "So you're a friend of Anouk's?"

He burst out laughing, "Why not? I live and work in Quebec."

At the moment, he had to leave, to catch a plane that evening, no time to get to know each other better, however . . . he pulled a business card from his wallet, she started speaking, words tumbling over each other, all the while thinking she should show some restraint, but he had to know, he must know. "I'm here to heal from the death of my son, just a few months ago . . . and to meet you."

He wrapped his arms around her, she left hers at her side, and the intensity of emotion emanating from him hit her full in the chest, robbing her of speech and breath.

Back from Dakota, a wonderful dream one night at
Hélène's in Montreal: she walked with her father, younger
by a few years, along a path lined with trees in full leaf.
A man in his thirties worked in a garden, he approached
them; she sensed that he and she were lovers. Then
she saw other horticulturalists, all good-looking, all in
their prime, cultivating dazzling flowers of all colours,
all kinds. Her young fiancé pulled her to a sheltered
spot hidden from view and bared her top, smiled, "Your
breasts even now are enough to take my breath away!"

Beneath his caress, she woke to the moist warmth
of her libido.

That morning, she rode the commuter train to clear
her head, find a new angle on her story, rid her mind of
clichés. Of course, she could always tell the tale as it had
happened, mourn what could have been and relegate it
to the past; impossible, however, since life got in the way.

There he stood in Central Station, the mystery man waiting for the same train. She'd pushed back her trip by an hour, not knowing that he would be waiting on the same platform; he had no idea that she had spotted him earlier on the crowded street and that she had hidden from view. She avoided him because of the longing he sparked in her, a burning, all-consuming desire, she didn't have the strength to look in his eyes and feel his touch, she felt like a moth singed once already by a candle's flame, knowing the fire could annihilate her. She fled, but he caught up to her anyway. They shared a seat, he spoke, asked how she'd been, whether she was handling her grief, if she was still painting, writing. Yes, yes, yes. Just a few simple words.

"How do you know that I write and paint?"

"Anouk told me."

He'd just returned from the North Shore and a stint as a stand-in doctor. He liked to get out of the city on exchanges with the regions, took public transit for the sake of the environment and because he was tired of driving and would rather be ferried around so he could work and not worry.

His eyes on hers shone, intense, dark, irresistible, like blazing stars, too bright, drawing her to him, a metal shard to his magnet. She felt both right and wrong in this inviolate space, wild and pure despite the men she and her body had known, struck by the realization that she had never loved with her entire being, no lover had ever penetrated the place she'd kept under lock since the actions of her father and brother. Until now, she had let love come to her unbidden, then said either yes or no.

He took her hand in his and held it there long enough for her to understand that their story would play out in the visible world. It was obvious to both of them, a certainty planted, an acknowledgement, she knew that when their time came, she would never leave him, when the stars and chance aligned to open the golden trail being traced at her back, she would turn to see him and walk with him to the end of their lifetime.

She decided to look on it as a feel-good story, a lifeline sent to her by the Mother of all creatures because it was not yet her time, a tasty carrot floated out front to keep her from falling or looking down into the mesmerizing, ever-tempting velvet of darkness.

He got off the train before her, her destination the end of the line, near a park she had strolled through one day with her grown child; they'd brought a picnic and a small ball they threw back and forth as they advanced, her son surprisingly agile, the two of them glad to be moving in unison.

She bade the church man good-bye with a chaste kiss, her lips barely pressed against his, no future encounter planned, no expectations, only grateful for their chance meeting. Two days later, she walked to the bookstore in her friend Hélène's neighbourhood to buy a dictionary of homonyms, her own left behind in Abitibi, when she spotted him chatting with the owner. She swore, then cried, *"Ben là?"* in her thickest Québécois accent, their laughter so infectious even the bookseller joined in, without knowing the reason for the moment's madness. He took her in his arms, gave her a big hug and invited her out for coffee. For the first time since her son's death, she was truly happy, there was so much joy in their meeting, such innocence that she let herself be won over and stopped resisting the call. He said, "This is what your son wants, for us to love each other, he's pulling the strings to his mother's happiness."

She recoiled, unwilling to involve her son's love in that of the mysterious stranger straight out of her dreams. He noticed and apologized for his blunder. Curious about his hard-to-place origins, she asked, "Where do you come from? Who are you?"

He gave a teasing smile, "I come from a Lakota grandmother — or Sioux if you prefer, she's who I got my crooked knife-edge of a nose from — who married a Franco-Manitoban. My other grandfather was Québécois, he met my grandmother on a beach in Florida; she was Afro-American, which explains the frizz in my hair! In other words, my parents are mixed blood, both part-American and part-Canadian. They met out in front of the White House, demonstrating against the Vietnam War, they were part of the beat generation . . ."

Worried, she asked, "Is there someone else in your life?"

His teasing air again, "Uh-huh, all kinds of people, but no one special woman. I've been divorced for too long and have never met the person who could make me fall for her . . . no children either. But since Dakota not a day has gone by that I haven't thought of you . . . The feeling that I know you somehow is so profound, it's very strange."

He added that he was as much a Lakota medicine man as a doctor.

His hand lay on her thigh, he leaned in; his breath on her neck, he inhaled deeply, his desire visible through the fabric of his pants.

They made their way to a small, quaint hotel surrounded by flowering trees. Their room opened onto the back courtyard, the decor tasteful and discreet. Intimidated, she became aware of the years separating the two of them, she on the cusp of her older years, he in the prime of his life. As she sat, she crossed her arms over her chest, trying without thinking to hide her age even though she was fully clothed. He came up to her and held out his hand, drew her toward the bed, invited her to lie down beside him, still dressed, so they could hold each other, feel the other's rhythm, each beating heart, the openness. All at once, she understood that this would be what she had always wanted for a first time; he held her gaze until he read total acceptance there, no longer the fear of not being good enough. He covered her face with gentle kisses, bringing a smile of consent to her lips. Then he kissed her, open-mouthed, his taste pleasing her, sweet like the mango juice he'd had in the café; she felt in a daze, in a dream. He undid the buttons on her blouse one by one, slowly, a ritual, unhooked her bra releasing her heavy breasts, brought his lips to her nipples, with his tongue drew gentle moans, then his voice sounded, "I love the fullness of your breasts, their shape, their softness . . ."

They undressed, his skin darker than hers, and she took pleasure in the dark-brown hand exploring her folds, her mature woman's curves, in love, yes, in love with her generous body greedy for more. He first tasting then entering her, their eyes locked. She lost herself in the long shimmering wave of an orgasm that propelled her past earthbound reality, heard from a distance his voice calling, worried and urgent, then her own sobs, like a tsunami, uncontrollable. He held her tight, his forehead cradled in the hollow of her shoulder shaken with spasms, wrapped his arms and legs around her. She knew he understood, was with her in the hurricane, her friend, her brother, her lover: death, suffering, the long, dreadful days of loneliness, life, love, joy, all were part of the whole, a full force explosion. Unbearable.

An artist friend invited her to accompany him to his opening. His art was representational but with a twist, splashes of red added to huge black-and-white drawings, a bloodstain on objects and figures. They got to the gallery early, he needed to speak to the owner before the guests arrived; she took her time walking through the exhibit to understand the reality underlying the artwork's seeming simplicity. He had ended with a paintball explosion. She suspected her friend had made no attempt to aim the gun, he must have worn a blindfold and shot as blind fate does, with no target, no emotion and, above all, no reason. Shooting for shooting's sake.

Glancing outside, she saw guests starting to park around the building then, from behind, caught sight of the church man studying a menu in the window of the restaurant across the street. He had been away for several weeks, travelling through northern communities and never knowing exactly when he'd return. Stunned, dazed, trembling, she found the only chair in the art gallery and lowered herself onto it, never losing sight of her lover's dark hair. Occasionally, passersby hid him from view for too long so she'd stand; she mustn't lose sight of him. Finally, he seemed to see what he wanted and stepped inside the restaurant. The artist emerged from the director's office and, seeing her approach him, asked what was wrong.

"I'm in love and I've just spotted my lover, I have to go."

He smiled. "Go then! You can introduce me!"

She ran down the sidewalk, clutching her purse to her belly, crossed the street, stepped into the restaurant and made her way slowly to his table. His face was half-hidden by the menu, which he seemed to be reading intently with a furrowed brow, ignoring the woman standing over him. When he finally looked up, he blanched, his dark skin turning grey, then joy flitted across his lips, dimples dug into his cheeks, his teeth shone in the dark of his face and his laughter swirled over the nape of her neck as he pulled her to him. Barely breathing in his embrace, she felt a flood of unexpected bliss and a moment's perfect happiness.

After that first intimate encounter, she'd written poetry, words consigned to pages she kept folded in a pocket of her purse. During the meal, they shared a rich, full-bodied bottle of wine; slightly tipsy she flitted from one subject to the next, as giddy as a fledgling in the sunshine of his presence. She said, "I have some poems for you . . . would you like to read them?"

Touched by his warmth, she unfolded the pages on the table. Unsure what he would think, she watched the pedestrians rushing past the window and caught an occasional glimpse of the art gallery full of guests with their raised wineglasses, talking and joking too by the way they threw back their heads and laughed. No sign of the artist. He had disappeared behind his crowd-studded success. The church man's voice cut through the momentary distraction, "Thank you . . . they're truly magnificent!"

He leaned over the plates and kissed her full on the mouth. Then clasped her hands in his. "I want to live with you, share your passions, your dreams . . ."

Caught off guard, she struggled to regain her balance: a quivering deep inside, the certainty of having reached a safe harbour after centuries of storms, of doubt about the meaning of it all, of suffering unspooling in private isolation that seemed to be life's lot, an awareness of the futility of this forced appearance on earth in such a fragile form. Flustered, it took her some time to pronounce the only words that made sense in this blessed moment, "I feel the same way. When the time is right, we'll be together."

She chose not to follow him home that night, too overwhelmed, succumbing to an urgent need for solitude and the warmth of the comforter in her room at Hélène's. Curled in the fetal position, exhausted, terrified by such a clear declaration of love, one she had thought not only inaccessible but, above all, incapable of existing, sheer wish fulfillment. But not only was the declaration real, he saw a future, a haven of peace in her, his partner in body, in heart, in spirit. He offered her the one thing she had ceased believing in, the one thing she no longer expected: the strength to continue on the path to the infinite with another.

The night was a sweltering greenhouse on this solstice, marking a summer so long delayed that young shoots froze underground until its abrupt appearance in compensation for its tardiness.

She had waited for the stillness of night to wend her way to the lake, the near full moon reflected in its dark mirror at the hour when earth's female spirits rose from the water for the time-honoured fertility ceremony.

Light lingered in a pale stain on the sky's western front; the day had been long, blistering, alive with rustling: in the wild grasses where crickets sang, in the forest where aspen trembled, their leaves mimicking the babbling of a joyous brook, and in the bushes where sparrows called to each other in unbridled trills, drunk with joy at heat's return.

That life could be so magnanimous after the cruelty of her descent into an inner, polar abyss astounded her; during that winter after her son's departure, she would often start trembling for no reason, grappling with a Siberian murmur in her lungs, shivering uncontrollably, brittle almost to the point of breaking with all the icicles hanging from the roof of her soul. Once, that spring after his departure, between two trips to the city, she traipsed down a path one rainy day, black mud clinging to her boots, letting the wind fray her fog of tears. No one within earshot to hear her cries. "Come get me! COME GET ME! I'VE HAD ENOUGH . . . enough . . . please!"

A flock of geese took wing from a pond hidden behind the trees and flew a few metres overhead in a gentle whoosh of wings and piercing cries. Then a hummingbird collided with her shoulder — not a simple brushing up against her, but a blow being struck — then hovered in front of her face, long enough to awaken wonder and amazement: the child loved hummingbirds.

A gift from her child whose arms of light wound round her on this day celebrating all mothers, even those who were mothers no longer, telling her to live.

She'd felt strong in body ever since the visit from her Italian friend whose golden hands had lain along her muscles, her nerves, her bones. She had succeeded where the best chiropractor had failed. Her back no longer ached, nor her head, she no longer bore her suffering in her flesh, it had been torn from her by the hands of the

woman life had placed along her path to ward off the
sacrifice she had believed must be made: that of carrying
out an act of liberation, entering the water to never return
on that most sacred night of nights, when darkness was
trounced by daylight; a night once devoted to love and
procreation in pagan times when sowing and the heat
of the sun were linked to the deities of fertility, but one
she had targeted to usher in another birth, hers, into
the invisible, to be with her luminous child once more.

Not long after, the church man had glided across
her skin.

So on that night when the women of earth remembered the goddess within, she no longer dreamed of
dying but of giving thanks to the winter child, to his
silence and presence among the birds and woods ringing
with song and the joyful hum emanating from all things
living and stirring still within the silken flesh of the
world. She threw away the doctor's pills she had been
saving for this special day chosen to join her child in
a place she imagined so full of peace that she would
no longer remember her sojourn among humankind.
Crouched on that rock plunging deep into the water,
her numbed body would have plummeted to the end
of the slope and sunk into the depths among the fish.

his voice

Live in peace, ma mère. You sleep next to the fragments
of my bones. You have planted a tree on my ashes to
watch over your dreams and to know I still live close by,
the guardian of your lands; but can't you feel me here,
as near as can be, in spirit but in your genes as well,
interwoven with your innermost self. I am your blood,
your heart, intimately linked to your hopes and dreams.

Live, *ma mère,* live with the wisdom passed down
from your ancestors. You feel guilt over my fate, I know,
but I had a choice as to which road to take, I alone am
responsible for the choice I made; to believe otherwise
would be to strip me of the clarity and intelligence I
embodied while still alive. The time spent in our bodies
is only one experience, *ma mère,* love is what we truly are;
I am able — even though time has ceased to exist in my
essence, in the space I inhabit — to tell you that much in
words so you can free yourself of us, of what we were for
each other, none of which counts anymore.

The wood is stacked, fire warms the house, from now on I am moulded by the orb of your shadow, where was I, my son, as you lay dying, coughing up blood?

Everything is alive: you would like to see sorrow suffer, howl in disgust at delighting in the wounds it inflicts on you, shoulder shame for the harm it is obliged to inflict on you; you lash out at the infinite nature of my disappearance, but you too belong to the infinite, from which we all come, and if you can find the strength to accept that I am gone without cursing creation, you will see your way to receiving the joy in store for you. When I come to you at night, I am real, more so than when I was alive for there are no barriers left, no bonds to protect, no secrets to keep, no hurt feelings enveloped in reason; I am light, freedom, no longer a being, I am life's essence, the breath of the universe. So no more tears, go and live.

I heard your suffering from behind a door I could not open, such sorrow still, my son.

I know what we shared, what you gave and what you took from us, your children. When you left us, your family, hiding the violence of your gesture behind the semblance of a parting on good terms with our father, you hurt me beyond words, beyond comprehension; you were my womb, the light at the heart of my daily questions about life, my outer limit when I rushed headlong toward forbidden cliffs, my trust in others. You betrayed me. Yes, you left our world broken so naturally I, too, could leave my world broken, giving into my sometimes stormy nature or unaware of the need to dial down my frustration. But you knew how bothered and embarrassed I was after every misplaced bout of anger, blowing in from I didn't know where . . . You had your reasons, maybe you missed out on childhood or adolescence, or didn't feel loved enough and sought the star that guides love's adventurers to the non-existent skies of utopia; or maybe you were simply tired of us fighting, shouting and shrieking, racing through the house and driving you mad, you who loves silence so much. Even as a child, I was strong enough to rip a door off its hinges, making you, my parents, wonder what kind of little monster you'd brought into the world . . .

The sun enters my house, insolent, blinds the books on the table, penetrates the rooms right through to the north door, its rays like a herd of luminous horses. It strikes my legs, bringing warmth, seems to bend to reach my cheeks, my eyes, my forehead.

The blue-tinged hills, the fields, the forests watch over your roof, even the snow safeguards the gentleness of the home you love for its remoteness, its distance from others, protected by the soft cloak of sky and stars. I didn't have

faith in my talent. I see you're thinking of the pictures
I drew of my cat and sold so successfully to neighbours.

You were twelve, my love, only twelve, don't forget!
You set up a table by the street and offered a free glass
of lemonade with every print sold: at the end of the day,
all your art was gone.

I loved music more than anything, but every time
my band had a show, I'd lose confidence and worry what
the audience would think of me; so I drank before each
performance, then got the notes wrong, just as I'd feared.
Eventually, my bandmates asked me to leave the group.
But you have always stuck to your path, *ma mère*, keep
holding fast.

I remember how hurt you were when your drawing
didn't win that contest . . .

The contest was for the whole elementary school, I
was six. My big sister found her inspiration in a painting
you were working on, a self-portrait, while I drew my
teddy bear freehand — you were amazed. I was convinced
I'd win, you were, too; I read the promise in your eyes.
My sister won the prize, and the art teacher phoned home
to make sure her pastel drawing wasn't done by you; you
were proud of my sister and sad for me. My life modelled
itself on that contest: I was just as talented at everything,
but shrouded by a veil I could never bring myself to tear

away to let in all the light. My sister wrote a story, a tale they made me study years later in French class for its perfection and insights.

The one time you came to visit me here with your sister and her family, you wore a long black wool overcoat; you were so handsome, your braid floating on the fabric. I looked for that elegant coat among the few clothes left behind in your apartment. It was there, at the back of the closet, dirty, wrinkled and balled up like an old rag. I asked your father to keep it for me; the overcoat hangs in my closet, clean again, smart. Minus you.

Acne disfigured me for so many years, the most vulnerable years, the teen years. You'd exclaim, "You're so handsome, my son!" And I'd be furious, thinking you were making fun of me. I suffered so much that nothing but food could calm me somewhat, I became fat. I was called "Pizza face," "Extra-large all-dressed," too. The day you told me I was obese and that it didn't look good on me, you robbed me of my appetite. Another powerful hurt on top of the acne. That period in my life levelled any confidence I might have had in my looks, even after the stringent treatment that erased all signs from my skin of the scaling ugliness and showed the world my true face. You were right to see past the oozing scarlet pustules on my flesh. Just as your absence was part of me, so was the hurt inflicted by others' words, seared into my soul with the red-hot irons of gratuitous cruelty. Later, I met the most beautiful girl in the world, but because I doubted myself, I turned into a sorry lapdog and she soon found love in someone else's arms.

I remember, you were little still, you'd just started grade school and the minute you got home at the end of the day, you'd grab your schoolbag to go work with your friend Martin, who was hopeless in school; no one made you do it, it was your own unprompted choice . . .

I did help him, but the truth is, he copied my homework, he couldn't make head or tail of either letters or numbers. You talk about my generosity, my big heart that got me into so much trouble because I could never say no to people living hand to mouth; I sometimes felt taken advantage of and that made me sad, but I'd still agree to help out. I loved it when you took me in your arms, moved by my good boy acts of kindness; even as a grown-up I sought your gaze, I was always the little boy waiting on his mother. I missed you horribly, so much so that I never grew inside; that tender, fragile spot curled up on itself the day I thought that, because you'd abandoned me, you no longer loved me. You know what I mean, you knew what I felt and your words weren't enough to fill the deep, dark pit you'd dug in my gut, not unlike the one you feel now I'm gone. But all things are relative, nothing is bad in and of itself, there is only life: we each have strengths and weaknesses and humankind can seem so absurd, so insane at times. Don't try to understand, instead live, walk toward the horizon you see each morning, be calm and serene, I repeat: I am with you and in you, I am part of your emotions and your flesh, more so than when I lived, I assure you, I'm at peace now, utterly free and content.

With my eyes closed, I saw you walking through the dark, dressed in black the way you always used to, leaning forward, striding across sombre skies toward a gap in the clouds, a light brighter than the sun. The moment, the sacred moment, arrived at last, and a silken warmth flooded my breast, irradiating my entire being.

You disappeared and left us the earth.

Virginia Pésémapéo Bordeleau is an internationally recognized visual artist and writer of Cree origin. She has published three novels, *Ourse bleue, L'amant du lac* and *L'enfant hiver,* and two poetry collections, *De rouge et de blanc* (honourable mention for the Télé-Québec award) and *Je te veux vivant.* An unpublished collection, "Le crabe noir," won the literary prize for poetry and the booksellers' prize for the Abitibi-Témiscamingue award for poetry. She makes her home in Abitibi. She has been invited to literary festivals in the Caribbean, Polynesian Islands and Europe with her novels and collections of poetry. As a visual artist, she was awarded the Regional Award of Excellence by Quebec's Conseil des arts et des lettres and her work has been exhibited in Canada and abroad.

Susan Ouriou is an award-winning writer and literary translator who has published over 20 book translations, as well as 15 co-translations with Christelle Morelli. Ouriou was awarded the Governor General's Award for Literary Translation in 2009 for *Pieces of Me*, and several of her translations have been featured on the honour list compiled by the International Board on Books for Youth (IBBY). Ouriou co-founded the Banff International Literary Translation Centre (BILTC) and has worked as faculty translating and interpreting for the Banff Centre's Aboriginal Emerging Writers (now Indigenous Writing) residency. She is also the author of a shortlisted novel, *Damselfish,* and a just-published young adult novel, *Nathan.*

Christelle Morelli is a French–English literary translator and teacher in the Francophone school system. She has translated the anthology *Languages of Our Land: Indigenous Poems and Stories from Quebec* and the children's book *Blanche Hates the Night,* as well as done over 15 co-translations with Susan Ouriou. Morelli and Ouriou's co-translation *Stolen Sisters: The Story of Two Missing Girls, Their Families and How Canada Has Failed Indigenous Women* was shortlisted for the Governor General's Literary Award for Translation in 2015.